Truth,
Dare, Kiss,
Promise

Teen
Queens

Cathy Hopkins is the author of the incredibly successful *Mates, Dates* and *Truth, Dare* books, and has recently started a fabulous new series called *Cinnamon Girl*. She lives in North London with her husband and three cats, Molly, Emmylou and Otis.

Cathy spends most of her time locked in a shed at the bottom of the garden pretending to write books but is actually in there listening to music, hippie dancing and talking to her friends on e-mail.

Occasionally she is joined by Molly, the cat who thinks she is a copy-editor and likes to walk all over the keyboard rewriting and deleting any words she doesn't like.

Emmylou and Otis are new to the household. So far they are as insane as the older one. Their favourite game is to run from one side of the house to the other as fast as possible, then see if they can fly if they leap high enough off the furniture. This usually happens at three o'clock in the morning and they land on anyone who happens to be asleep at the time.

Apart from that, Cathy has joined the gym and spends more time than is good for her making up excuses as to why she hasn't got time to go.

Cathy Hopkins

Truth, Dare, Kiss, Promise

Teen Queens

Piccadilly Press • London

*Thanks as always to Brenda Gardner, Yasemin Uçar and the
ever fab team at Piccadilly. To Rosemary Bromley at Juvenilia. And to
Georgina Acar, Scott Brenman, Becca Crewe, Alice Elwes,
Jenni Herzberg, Rachel Hopkins and Olivia McDonnell for
answering all my questions about what it's like being a teenager these days.*

First published in Great Britain in 2003
by Piccadilly Press Ltd,
5 Castle Road, London NW1 8PR

This edition published 2008

A catalogue record for this book is available from
the British Library

ISBN: 978 1 85340 969 1 (paperback)

3 5 7 9 10 8 6 4 2

Printed in the UK by CPI Bookmarque, Croydon, CR0 4TD
Typeset by M Rules, London
Set in Garamond and Fineprint
Cover design by Simon Davis
Cover illustration by Susan Hellard

Mixed Sources
Product group from well-managed
forests and other controlled sources
FSC   www.fsc.org   Cert no. TT-COC-002227
© 1996 Forest Stewardship Council

Valentine's Day

'POST IS HERE, Lia,' Mum called as she went past my bedroom.

I looked out of the window to see the post van zooming away down the drive to the left of the house. It was a lovely clear day and the view from my window was stunning. Terraced lawns, then acres of fields leading down to the sea and our private beach. Although I've been officially living at home for almost eight months now, opening my curtains in the morning is still a thrill and such a change from the apartment block that I looked out on when I was at boarding school up in London.

'Be right down,' I called back, then went into my bathroom to find my make-up bag. I wasn't in any great hurry to go downstairs. Not today. It was Friday, February 14th. Valentine's Day. That meant cards and I knew there wouldn't be any for me.

As I slicked on some lip-gloss, I thought back to this time last year when I was still a boarder. I'd got loads of cards then. I had loads of boyfriends too. Jason, Max, Elliott, Leo, Edward. None of them were major or soulmates or anything serious, just part of the gang that used to hang out together. But there had been dates. And cards. We'd send them to each other just for a laugh or so that no one missed out.

Life is so different since I moved down here to Cornwall. New school, new friends, new everything apart from romance. Not one single date since I changed schools. Hence the lack of expectation when it came to Valentine's cards.

I pottered around in my room getting ready for school, then my curiosity got the better of me. Maybe there'd be one card from some mysterious stranger who was secretly pining for me. An admirer who will later reveal himself to be the next best thing since pecan fudge ice cream. Yeah, and there's a yeti living in my fridge, I thought as I grabbed my rucksack and headed downstairs.

Mum was sorting through a pile of envelopes at the counter in the kitchen when I got down. She glanced up and by the look in her eyes, I could tell that I'd been right. Nothing for me.

'It's cool,' I said. 'I wasn't expecting any.'

Mum shook her head. 'They all need their heads examining, these boys down here.' She pointed at a jug on the counter. 'I've just made some juice. Beetroot, orange and raspberry. Help yourself.'

'Um, think I'll stick with plain orange,' I said going to the fridge and helping myself to a carton.

Juicing is one of Mum's passions – partly for health reasons, partly for beauty. She's forty, but only looks thirty, which she puts down to juicing. She says it takes years off people and improves their skin no end. Some of her concoctions are fab, but some of them are strange with a capital S. I looked over at the dark crimson liquid in the juicer. 'You're not going to serve that at the party tonight, are you?'

Mum laughed. 'No. Course not. We'll be having Bellinis as the theme is Venetian.'

'That's champagne and peach juice, isn't it?' I knew because my sister Star likes them. She always has a bottle of champagne and a carton of peach juice in the fridge in her tiny flat in Notting Hill. She makes me laugh as sometimes that's *all* she has in her fridge and, when I go to stay with her, I have to go and buy proper food myself. It's not that Star doesn't eat, she does, it's just that she eats out most of the time and is hardly ever home.

Mum nodded. 'There's a place near St Mark's Square in Venice called Harry's Bar. It's famous for its Bellinis.'

'Harry's Bar? Doesn't sound very Italian. Sounds more like a café in the East End of London.'

'I know,' said Mum. 'But then there's probably a famous café in the East End called La Dolce Vita that sells the best cup of tea in the city.'

I laughed. Mum was in her element planning parties. If she ever had to work, that would be her perfect job as she's always throwing a do or planning the next. Always over the top. Always with a theme and always no expense spared. This time, the party planners have been here for weeks recreating Venice for a masked ball to be held in a marquee in the top acre of the garden. I felt like I was living in a hotel with all the catering vans outside and people buzzing about carrying vast flower arrangements, swathes of fabric or lights.

'Any cards there for the Cornish Casanova?' I asked.

The Cornish Casanova is my elder brother, Ollie. He boards at school up in London, but he comes back about once a month and has a long list of admirers down here, including my mate, Cat.

Mum counted the cards. 'Three. But most girls know to send his to his school as he's there in the week.'

'I guess,' I said. 'In fact, the post office probably had to hire an extra van to cope with the load addressed to him.' Ollie's always been a girl magnet. He's got Mum's great bone structure and blue eyes but with dark hair like Dad, not blonde like Mum and me. As I drank my juice, I wondered if Cat had sent a card to him. She and Ollie have had a bit of a 'thing' since last summer. Nothing official, but you can see that they're really into each other whenever they're together. She knows that he's commitment-phobic so doesn't expect too much. I think that's one of the things that he likes about her and why she's lasted so long. She's cool about him, whereas other girls have virtually camped on his door to try and pin him down. Perfect way to get him to back off, which is why Cat is playing it just right.

'I got one from Dad.' Mum smiled as she put an enormous flowery card on the kitchen counter. 'And he's got his usual sack full.'

My dad is Zac Axford, lead singer of the rock band Hot Snax. They were big in the eighties and he still has a bunch of faithful followers who never forget him, even though most of them are in their forties now. I tease him that he's like Cliff Richard with his middle-aged fan club, but with his faded rock star looks, his tatty jeans, leather jackets and shoulder length hair, he's more Mick Jagger than Cliff.

I went out into the hall, grabbed my jacket and went to wait outside for Meena, our housekeeper, to bring the Mercedes round to take me to school. Max and Molly, our mad red setters, came bounding up with their usual morning greeting of licks and paws on the shoulder. At least you love me, I thought as Max almost knocked me off my feet.

I couldn't help but feel disappointed that there wasn't

one card for me even though I'd told myself that there wouldn't be. Get over it, it's no biggie, I told myself. So I haven't got a boyfriend down here, so what? At least I've made good mates – Cat, Becca, Mac and Squidge. They're really cool, though different to the London crowd in that their relationships seem to be more long-term. Becca has been going out with Mac for about six months, and Cat went out with Squidge for a few years until they broke up last summer, when she fell under the spell of the Cornish Casanova. The longest that I or any of my London mates ever lasted in a relationship was about three months. No one wanted to get tied down to one person.

Still, this new crowd have been brilliant and have made me feel really welcome. I felt petrified that first day of term last year and began to wonder if I'd made a huge mistake asking to change school. It wasn't that I didn't like my old school, I did, and I had great mates there – Tara, Athina, Gabby, Sienna, Isobel, Olivia and Natalie. It was after Mum and Dad bought the house down here that everything changed. I had to be a boarder and as my mates were all day pupils, it was a bit lonely some evenings. On top of that, getting home at the weekend was a long way to travel. I felt like I never saw Mum and Dad properly, as I was forever on a train going back and forth. It didn't bother Ollie. He wanted to stay as a boarder, but I told Mum I'd like to go to a local school and live at home. She didn't object or try and talk me out of it, not even for a second, as I think she missed me as much as I missed her. She spoke to the headmistress down here and it was agreed. I'd move after Year Eight.

When I got to the new school, everyone seemed to know each other so well, all chatting and catching up after the summer, all totally familiar with where classes were, who the teachers were, who their mates were. And then there was me, the new girl in Year Nine, wondering where I fitted, if anywhere. All the cliques and friendships had clearly been established long ago and I wondered if I was destined to be a loner for the whole year, standing on the outside looking in. Not my favourite time, plus I really missed all the old gang back in London. Cat was my saviour. She offered to show me around the school and we clicked immediately. She's one of the nicest, most genuine, unpretentious people I've ever met. Her mum died when she was nine and I think it made her grow up over night. Whatever, it's made her sensitive to people when they're a bit lost, maybe on account of feeling lost herself when her mum first went.

I heard the car toot outside the garages, so I took a deep breath and prepared myself for the inevitable inquisition at school.

2 Mystery Admirer?

EVERYONE WAS hanging out in the corridor by the assembly hall when I got in. All the talk was about the school Valentine's disco and cards, with lots of whispering, giggling and secret looks as people tried to guess who'd sent which card to who and who'd left which card in whose locker or rucksack.

'So, how many did you get?' asked Becca.

'Oh, way too many to count,' I replied, trying to laugh it off. I started to count on my fingers. 'One from Robbie Williams, one from Tobey Maguire, one from . . .'

Becca's eyes widened. 'Really?'

Cat punched her arm. 'No, she's kidding you.'

I laughed. Becca was so gullible. She thinks that because Dad's in the music business that we know everyone. 'How many cards did you get, Bec?'

'Just one, I guess it's from Mac,' said Becca, as she pulled her long red hair into a ponytail. 'At least it better had be seeing as I sent him one. What about you, Cat?'

'One. Don't know who it's from. At first, I thought it was from Squidge as we've sent each other cards for years, but it's not his writing. I'd know his scrawl even if he tried to disguise it.'

'I think people ought to sign Valentine's cards,' said Becca. 'It would save a lot of grief knowing who they were from.'

'They do in some places,' I said. 'One of my mates at my old school was American and she said that sometimes they sign them there.'

'Yeah, but it would take the mystery out it,' said Cat. 'It's fun trying to guess.'

'Did you send Squidge a card?' I asked.

Cat shook her head. 'It's not like that with us any more.'

'Did you send Ollie one?'

'Nah. I reckon his head's big enough as it is and no doubt he'll get a sack-load despite me. But seriously, Lia, how many did you get?'

I made my finger and thumb into an O.

'I don't get it,' said Cat. 'I mean, look at you. You're *stunning*, tall, long blonde hair, silver-blue eyes . . . you're most boys' fantasy girl! Boys visibly dribble when you enter a room, and no, don't shake your head, I've *seen* them. By my reckoning, half the school is madly in love with you.'

'Yeah, but some of the boys here like to act really hard,' said Becca. 'You know, they think that they'd look like soppy Sarahs if they did anything remotely romantic like send a card. Pathetic, isn't it? Doesn't mean that you haven't got loads of boys interested in you, though, Lia.'

'So why haven't I had one single date since I got here then?'

'Beneath the hard act, most boys are chickens,' said Becca. 'They're intimidated. You're beautiful, a five-star babe and most of them know that they're not in your league. Boys hate rejection more than anything, so I reckon most of them daren't ask you out for fear of being turned down.'

'I agree,' said Cat. 'Anyway, you're not missing much. Our school isn't exactly Talent City.'

Becca punched Cat's arm. 'Er, excuse me. Mac?'

'Yeah, course,' said Cat. 'And Squidge, but I don't count them. They're mates.'

I didn't say anything, but privately, I think I could fancy Squidge if I let myself. But I don't go there seeing as Cat and he were an item for ages and they're still really close mates. I don't know how she'd feel about me being into Squidge and I don't want to mess up anything between us. So I'm happy to just be good friends with him. Besides, I don't think I'm his type. I'm tall and blonde and Cat is petite and dark, plus he's never given the slightest indication that he feels the same way about me.

'There's always Jonno Appleton,' said Becca glancing at a tall boy with spiky dark hair from Year Eleven, who was standing by the doors. 'He's a nine out of ten in anybody's book.'

'Yeah,' I said, 'I do fancy him, but who doesn't? Anyway, he's taken by Rosie Crawford, so it's hands off. Boyfriend stealing is against my rules.'

'What do we care?' said Cat. 'Isn't Ollie bringing that Michael guy down from London with him tonight?'

I felt my face flush. 'Yeah. Michael Bradley.'

'Does Ollie know that you like him?' asked Becca.

'No way,' I said. 'And you mustn't say anything. I'd die. No, I'd *never* tell Ollie as he might think he could do me a favour or something and try and fix us up. No, I want it to happen naturally.'

I've known Michael since I was knee-high and had a crush on him since I was seven. Not that he's ever noticed me, not in a big way. I'm just Ollie's kid sister, someone to thrash at tennis and throw in the swimming pool in summer. But tonight I intend to change all that. We haven't seen each other for nearly a year and when Ollie told me that he was bringing him down for Mum's party, my imagination went into overdrive. My plan was to persuade Ollie to come with Michael to the school disco with the rest of us. That way, I could show Michael off a bit and prove to the school that I am not *totally* repulsive to boys. Then later at Mum's do . . . well, who knows what a romantic night in Venice might bring?

When the last bell went in the afternoon, school emptied in a flash. Doubtless everyone had their plans. Home, shower, dress, make-up, back to school. Our plan was to meet at Cat's, get dressed there, go to the school disco for an hour or so, then up to my house for Mum's latest extravaganza. She said that I could invite anyone I liked from school, but I'd only invited Becca, Cat, Squidge and Mac.

It's funny, but since I came down here, sometimes I feel a bit awkward about how rich my family are. It's like I don't want anyone to think I'm showing off or flaunting it. All I've ever wanted was to be normal and be accepted and that was easy at my old school because most people's parents were loaded or famous. There was even a princess in Year Ten. Down here, though, people aren't as well off and sometimes all they see are the flash cars, the big house and my dad's fame. What they don't know is that Mum and Dad lead very quiet lives most of the time. Both of them are real homebodies. Mum loves nothing better than pottering in the garden growing herbs and vegetables and Dad is happiest in his studio listening to sounds or watching the telly. But that's not what the public see. They see Dad on telly whenever he does interviews, which is rarely these days. Or in videos on MTV. They think that he's the wild man of rock and roll. The Cornish Ozzy Osbourne. I can't help being his daughter, and down here, I want to be Lia Axford – not Lia, Zac Axford, famous rock star's daughter. There's a difference, and sometimes it gets in the way of people's perception of me at my new school. I guess that's why I try to keep my family history quiet and in the background, so to speak.

I raced home to pick up my clothes to take to Cat's. It was complete pandemonium when I got there with even more people dashing about than there had been in the morning. The Venetian theme had really taken shape. A trio of musicians were rehearsing in the hall and there were ornate candelabras in the corridor leading to the right of the house where the marquee had been set up for the party. It's going to look really fab, I thought as I spotted Mum giving a group of caterers some last minute instructions.

'Is Ollie back?' I asked her.

She nodded her chin towards the stairs. 'In his room with his friends, and oh, Lia, I'll leave a selection of masks in your room for you and your friends to put on when you're back from the school disco. Don't be back too late, OK?'

'OK. Thanks, Mum,' I said. Ollie's with his friends? Who else besides Michael, I wondered as I took the stairs two at a time. Never mind, the more, the merrier. I made a quick dash up to my room to brush my hair and spritz some Cristalle on before going to say hello and hopefully get Michael to notice me properly for the first time.

As soon as I opened my door, I noticed a blue envelope on my bed. My name had been written on it in beautiful handwriting. I ripped it open. It was a card with a red rose on it. Inside, it read: *To the girl with silver eyes, from a distant admirer who's waiting until the time is right to reveal himself. Happy Valentine's.* Then three kisses.

I felt a rush of excitement as I studied the envelope for clues. No stamp, so it must have been either delivered by hand or come from someone in the house.

Hmmm. Interesting, I thought as I heard Ollie and Michael's voices in the corridor outside.

Disco

3

'HEY, IF it isn't little Lia,' said Michael when I opened my bedroom door. Then he looked me up and down. 'Only not so little any more. You've shot up in the last year. You look great!'

'Thanks,' I said and gave him my best flirty look. So far, so good, I thought as he enveloped me in a huge hug. He looked as gorgeous as I remembered – tall and dark, with velvety brown eyes and amazing chiselled features.

'All ready for tonight?' asked Ollie. 'Is Cat coming?'

'Yeah. Later with me. First we've got to go to our school disco. In fact, I wondered if you and Mich . . .' At that moment, I heard the door of one of the guest rooms open and close behind us and as I turned, a girl with long dark hair was coming towards us. She was very pretty – Indian-looking, with lovely high cheekbones. Oh *no*, I thought. Ollie's brought one of his 'girlfriends' with him. I hope

Cat's not going to be upset. I felt a flash of annoyance. He *always* does this. Keeps himself surrounded with different girls, so that no one can get too close to him.

'Lia, this is Usha,' said Ollie as the girl came to join us. 'Michael's girlfriend.'

As she slipped her hand into Michael's, I tried to smile and look friendly, but inside, I felt like my chest was made of glass and someone had just shattered it. 'Oh . . . er, hi Usha.'

'So what were you just saying?' asked Ollie. 'Something about a disco?'

'Yeah. Got to dash. Disco at school. Going there first. Be back later. See you then.'

I ran back to my room, locked the door, dived on to my bed and put my pillow over my head. Girlfriend? He'd brought his *girlfriend*! Stinking finking. I never saw that coming. But, of course, someone as attractive as Michael was bound to have a girlfriend and Ollie wasn't to know that I fancied him. I lay on my bed for a while, stared at the ceiling and ran through all the swear words I knew in my head. I daren't say them out loud as there were too many people in the house and someone might be passing my room and think I'd gone mad. Suddenly I wasn't in the mood for a disco, or a party. I wanted to hide under my bed and come out when it was all over.

A moment later, Cat phoned to ask if she could borrow my red beaded choker and it all came tumbling out.

'. . . so, you see, I just can't come,' I said. 'I'd be lousy company and . . .'

'So what are you going to do? Hide in your bedroom all night? You know you can't do that. Your mum or someone's bound to come up and drag you out, then you'll have to spend the whole night watching Michael with Usha. No, come on, Lia, best get out of there. Take your mind off it. And you never know, we might have a good time at school, then later, at least Bec, Mac, Squidge and I will be there with you.'

The school disco was well underway by the time we got there. In the end, it wasn't me who held us up but Becca. She took six changes of clothes to Cat's and couldn't decide what to wear. She finally decided on black trousers and a black handkerchief top. She looked really sophisticated, more eighteen than fourteen.

Cat wore her short red dress and my choker and looked lovely as always. The name Cat suits her as she looks a bit like a cat – dark, glossy and serene. Mum and I had picked out a silvery coloured mini-dress with sparkles on it last time we were up in London, but it seemed a bit OTT for the school disco. I wasn't in the mood for dressing up, so I just put on my jeans and a pale blue halter-neck top instead.

'You'd look good whatever you wore,' said Becca as we

tried to apply lip-gloss beneath the glaring fluorescent lights in the girls' cloakroom at school. I couldn't help thinking how different it looked to back home where Mum had put jasmine scented candles, flowers and Floris soaps in all the cloakrooms. The only aroma here was the pong of disinfectant that the cleaners used to scour the loos with.

As we stood in front of the mirrors doing our hair, Kaylie O'Hara came in with one of her mates, Susie Cooke. Cat gave me an 'Oh, here we go' look as Kaylie is one of those girls who takes over a place even if it's only the cloakroom. It's as if when she arrives, no one else is important. She has to be the centre of attention and she's certainly very popular, especially with the boys. Becca says it's because boys are breast-fixated and she has the largest chest in our year. She always wears very tight tops that make her boobs look as though they're straining to escape. She's easily the prettiest of her group, in a baby-doll kind of way, and her mates are all clones of her. There are four of them. Kaylie, Susie, Jackie and Fran. Becca calls them the Barbies. Cat calls them the Clones. All of them are really girlie girls who have blonde highlighted hair that they flick around a lot. They all wear loads of shiny lip-gloss which they are always reapplying, even in the middle of maths. And lately, they've all started talking in this lispy breathy voice. Kaylie started it a few weeks ago and now they all do it. I guess they think it makes them sound sexy, but I think it makes them sound silly. Cat says Kaylie and her mates are as thick as two short planks. In her usual subtle way (not), Becca thinks that they will all probably marry some very rich but stupid men. 'The type that likes arm candy, but doesn't care that the candy is braindead.'

'Tonight's the night,' sang Kaylie as she headed for the mirror next to us and began to apply pink gloss to her lips.

'You look happy,' said Becca.

Kaylie winked at Susie. '*Indeed.* Just heard some interesting news. Some *very* interesting news.'

'Come on, then,' said Becca, who never held back when she wanted to know something. 'Spill.'

Kaylie smiled. 'Ah, well . . .' Then she began singing again. 'Tonight's the night . . .'

Becca shrugged and headed for the door.

'Oh, all right,' pouted Kaylie. 'You'll find out soon enough anyway.' She folded her arms and leaned back against the sink. 'Jonno Appleton's broken up with Rosie.'

'Is *that* all?' said Becca. 'So what's the big deal?'

'He's free, you eejit,' she said then raised an eyebrow, 'but not for long if I have my way.'

Cat shot me a look as if to say, Yeah right, then turned to Kaylie. 'But sometimes people need a bit of space when they've just split up with someone. He may not be ready yet.'

Kaylie tapped the side of her nose. 'Oh, don't worry. I

know how to play it. I have it all worked out, in fact. I have an ickle plan.'

I guess I must have let out a sigh when she said that, as she turned to look at me. 'You don't think I can do it?' she asked in a tight voice.

'No, I . . . it wasn't that . . .' I blustered. I didn't mean to dismiss her. I was just thinking that getting off with Michael had fizzled out despite all *my* plans. But I wasn't going to tell her about that. I felt intimidated by Kaylie. She's one of those girls who acts friendly, but you get the feeling that if you said the wrong thing, she could turn nasty. I've never crossed her, but I've seen her be really sarcastic to a couple of girls in our class. Luckily, she seemed to be in a good mood tonight.

'Whatever,' she said as she took out a can of hairspray and sprayed liberally around her head. Some of the spray hit me in the eye. 'Oh *sorry,* Lia, did I get you? Oops.'

'S'OK,' I said as I rubbed my eye. I swear she did it on purpose, but there was no way I was going to say anything.

Kaylie stood back and looked at her reflection. 'Tonight, Mr Appleton, you are mine, *all* mine.'

Susie laughed and flicked her hair back. 'He doesn't stand a chance, poor guy.'

At that moment, Annie Peters came in and stood next to Kaylie at the sink. I like Annie. She's in Year Eleven and is a bit of an oddball. She does her own thing, has her own hippie style and is brilliant at art, particularly photography.

'Hey, nice watch,' she said to Kaylie as she applied some moss-green kohl to her eyes.

Kaylie beamed. 'Thanks. It's a Cartier.'

'For real?' asked Annie, taking Kaylie's wrist.

'Yeah, course. My brother brought it back from Thailand for me. Cool, huh?'

Annie examined the watch and nodded. 'Yeah. Nice. There's one sure way to tell if it's real, though.'

'How?' asked Kaylie as I headed for the door. Now would be a good time to leave, I thought as I had the same watch on. My dad got it for me last Christmas and I've no doubt that mine's real, as I was with him when he bought it from the Cartier shop in London.

'Easy,' said Annie. 'My dad got my mum one for their twentieth wedding anniversary. She said that you can tell a real Cartier by looking at one of the numbers, I think it's the V, under a magnifying glass. If it's genuine, you can see the word Cartier written in minuscule writing.'

I gave Becca the nod to say let's go, but she clearly wanted to stay and watch what was happening. Annie rummaged in her bag. 'I've got a magnifying glass in here somewhere. Let's have a look.'

She pulled out her glass, held it close to Kaylie's wrist, then screwed her eyes up to look at the watch. 'Nope. Can't see any word.'

I thought it was a bit mean of Annie to humiliate Kaylie like that, as she'd obviously been chuffed thinking that she had a real Cartier. To me, it's no big deal. A watch is a watch, main thing is that it tells the time, but I wanted to say something to make Kaylie feel better. 'It looks real to me,' I said. 'It might just be on a particular model that the V has Cartier written on it.' Big mistake as all eyes turned to me. Eagle-eyes Annie spotted my watch straight away.

'Hey, same watch,' she said, before I could hide my arm behind my back. 'What a coincidence. Here. Let's have a look at yours, Lia.'

Quick as a flash, she had my wrist in her hand and was scrutinising my watch. 'Yep,' she said. 'Here it is. Tiny. Cartier. Want to look, Kaylie?'

'Think I'll pass,' she said sulkily as she flounced towards the door. 'Little things for little minds.'

'Good luck with Jonno,' I called after her, in an attempt to break the sour atmosphere.

'Yeah, whatever,' she said. Then she smiled back at me. But it was with her mouth not her eyes. She may be pretty, I thought, but there's something hard about her. She's clearly not someone to get on the wrong side of.

The music was thumping in the hall where the disco was being held. Already people were up, dancing and having a good time and the atmosphere was infectious. I soon forgot the incident in the cloakroom, as Becca and Cat pulled me out on to the floor and we began to dance. Mac and Squidge soon came to join us and after a while I began to really enjoy myself. Squidge is a brilliant dancer when he wants to be, but he was in the mood for looning about by doing Hawaiian dancing, then Greek, then Egyptian, then Russian – complete with knee bends and kicks. Then he fell over.

'And now, so that the teachers don't feel left out, we'll have a golden oldie session,' said the DJ. 'Here's a blast from the past for the wrinklies with an old Beatles number – "Can't Buy Me Love".'

The group of teachers, who were standing by the drinks table, smiled wearily then carried on chatting.

As we danced to the words, 'Money can't buy me love', I thought, that's so true. Money can't buy a good time either. Like there in the hall. The decorations looked really tatty. There were a few token balloons scattered around the walls and an old faded glitter ball catching light on the ceiling, and that was it, but it hadn't stopped anyone having a great time. Probably cost about five quid, I thought, whereas Mum's party must have cost thousands.

After a few dances, we went to get a drink and Becca nudged me. 'Over there,' she whispered. 'Kaylie gets her man.'

'Or not,' said Cat as she looked over. 'I think it's going to be a no score.'

I glanced over to where they were looking and saw Kaylie at the other end of the drinks table. She was desperately trying to get Jonno's attention, but he seemed more interested in talking to one of his mates from the football team. She was flicking her hair and sticking her chest out for all she was worth, but he wasn't taking any notice. When another Beatles track began to play, she pulled on his arm and tried to get him to join her on the dance floor, but he shook his head and turned away to get a drink.

That makes two of us let down by love today, I thought, feeling sorry for her for a moment.

Cat, Becca and I downed an orange juice then headed back on to the floor to join Mac and Squidge, who by now had moved on to sixties go-go dancing, *à la* Austin Powers style. We joined in and were having a real laugh when someone tapped me on the shoulder. I turned to see a handsome face smiling down at me.

'Want to dance?' asked Jonno Appleton.

Over his shoulder, I could see Kaylie watching from the drinks table. She didn't look pleased.

Party Time 4

WE LEFT the disco around ten o'clock and piled into Squidge's dad's van. He was great at ferrying us all around when we needed a lift.

'You don't mind roughing it, do you?' asked Mr Squires as he spread an old blanket that stank of petrol on the floor in the back.

I wedged myself in between a tool box and Becca. 'No, course not. Rough is the new smooth, don't you know?'

'Bet you never travelled like this up in London,' said Becca.

'Yeah, course I did,' I lied. I didn't want Squidge or his dad to think I was snobby about the van. I wasn't bothered at all, but the truth was, at my old school, everyone used cabs to get about. One night, my friend Gabby's dad even had his chauffeur pick us up and take us to the theatre in their Bentley. It was really cool. Her dad's a politician and the car had tinted windows and was bullet proof, at least Gabby said it was. Either way, we felt like we were in a Bond movie.

Mac jumped in and sat back against Becca pretending that she wasn't there. 'Er, seats are a bit lumpy, mate,' he joked to Squidge.

'Gerroff,' said Becca, pushing him off and into Cat who was squashed up in the corner.

'Gerroff yourself,' she said, pushing him back at Becca.

Mac made his body go limp and lay over both of them. 'Ah, poor me. At the mercy of cold-hearted women again.'

'Get in the front beside me, nutter,' Squidge laughed.

Mac climbed out, then closed the back door on us before getting in beside Squidge in the front.

What a strange night, I thought. In fact, what a strange day. No Valentine's card, then a card appears on my bed. I still don't know who sent it, but I guess Michael is off the list now. Probably Mum. It's the sort of thing she'd do. No boy interested in me, then the most popular boy in school makes a beeline for me. I had one dance with Jonno and he was really flirty, putting his arms around my waist and stuff, but I was so aware of Kaylie's eyes boring into me that I couldn't let go and enjoy it. In the end, I made an excuse and went back to mad dancing with my mates.

'You're bonkers,' said Becca as the van reached our driveway and the gates swung open. 'Jonno's *gorgeous*.'

'I know,' I said, 'but I don't want any trouble. Kaylie bagged him in the loos. You heard her.'

'So what? It doesn't mean that they're an item,' continued Becca. 'Anyone could see that he wasn't interested in her. He only had eyes for you.'

I shook my head. 'Not worth the aggro. I don't want to get on the wrong side of her.'

Becca sighed. 'Tough for her, I say. You can't let girls like Kaylie O'Hara run your life. Look at what *you* want to happen, not what she wants.'

'Yeah . . . I will,' I said. 'In fact, at the disco, I invited a few boys from Year Eleven up to the party.'

'Really?' said Cat. 'Who? Jonno?'

'No. Not Jonno. Seth and Charlie from your class, Squidge.'

'Yeah. They're OK,' he said from the front. 'Do you fancy one of them?'

'No. But I thought I ought to at least make an effort to be friendly to some new boys. New start, new chapter and all that.' I'd decided back at the disco that it was time I got to know some of the local boys a bit better, especially as all my stupid dreams about Michael had fallen through.

'In that case,' said Mac. 'No better way to make a new start than with a quick round of Truth, Dare, Kiss or Promise . . .'

'Oh *nooo*,' groaned Cat. 'It always gets us into trouble of some sort.'

27

'Oh, let's play,' said Becca, then she grinned. 'Only, because it's Valentine's day, you only have one option: Kiss. Sorry.'

'So, who do we have to kiss, Cupid?' asked Cat.

'And don't say I have to kiss Seth or Charlie, please,' I said.

'Well, Mac, you have to kiss me and I have to kiss you,' said Becca. 'Um, Cat, I'll make it easy for you, you have to kiss Ollie.'

Cat smiled. 'No problemo.'

'Now. What about Squidge?' asked Becca.

'How about I choose for myself in my own time,' he said. 'I don't like to rush these things. Let me think about it.'

I was about to say, Me too, I want to choose in my own time as well, when Becca piped up. 'OK, but Lia *has* to kiss Jonno Appleton.'

'No, oh come on, don't be a wind-up,' I said.

Becca shook her head. 'Sorry, it's been decided. If you're going to be such a wimp as to be intimidated by Kaylie, then you need a push from us. All those in favour of Lia snogging Jonno, raise your hands.'

Mac, Cat and Becca raised their hands.

'You should let her choose herself,' said Squidge as we reached the top of the drive.

'Sorry, you're out-voted, Squidge. Lia, did you or did you not say that you fancied Jonno Appleton?' demanded Becca.

'Yeah, but pick someone else, please . . .'

'Well, who else do you fancy?' demanded Becca as Mr Squires slowed the van down and parked between a Porsche and a BMW.

There was no way I was going to admit that I secretly liked Squidge. 'No one, really.'

'So the only boy you think is fanciable is Jonno, then?'

'I suppose,' I said, then looked at Mac and Squidge, who are both very good looking in their own ways. Mac is blond, with fine features and Squidge has brown, spiky hair, an open and friendly face, and a gorgeous, wide, smiley mouth, 'present company excepted, of course.'

'So that's settled, then,' said Becca. 'Better to kiss someone you actually like than being dared to go and kiss some reject. It will be fine, Lia. Live dangerously.'

'OK, but I'll do it in my own time,' I said.

'Fine,' said Becca, then grinned. 'You've got ten minutes. No, only joking. In your own time.'

Cat gave me a half smile and looked at Becca as if to say, What can you do? I smiled back. Sometimes you can't argue with Becca. And it might not be so bad if I could get Jonno on his own some time.

Mum had laid out some amazing masks on my bed for us.

'And there's more downstairs in the hall,' I said. 'Mum put a basket of them out by the fireplace for guests who didn't bring one.'

'No, these are brilliant,' said Becca holding up a silver mask to her face in the mirror.

The girls chose the pretty ones. Becca opted for one with a full white face with delicate gold sequinned patterning on the cheeks, gold lips and gold curls made out of paper around the head. Cat also went for a full face mask with red and gold diamond shapes painted on the cheeks, green rhinestones around the eyes and a red feather plume. Squidge chose a black half mask with a hooked nose. As he was wearing his long black leather coat, the combination with the mask made him look pretty sinister. Not to be outdone, Mac picked a scary one as well – red with a bird's beak nose. It didn't look as effective as Squidge's, as Mac was wearing a fleece and jeans. I picked a Pierrot mask. White with sad eyes, red lips and a tear painted on one cheek. Somehow it seemed to fit the mood of the day. It seemed I'd never be with a boy I liked. The beautiful Michael was attached, getting involved with the lovely Squidge was way too complicated and to respond to Jonno would only cause trouble. Yes, the Pierrot mask would be perfect.

When we were ready, we headed down and out to join the party. Most of the guests had already arrived as it was almost eleven o'clock and as we made our way through them, it was hard to tell who was who.

'Woah,' exclaimed Mac as he took in the sumptuous

decorations in the marquee. It did look fabulous – like stepping into another world where everything was red and gold. Mum had really surpassed herself. Soft candlelight lit the tented room and the trio of musicians dressed in eighteenth century costumes were playing classical music in a corner. Swathes of silk were draped around pillars and huge arrangements of flowers and grapes adorned every table. The whole effect was rich and romantic. There was even an ice sculpture of a lion with vodka coming out of it's mouth.

The classical trio finished playing their pieces and it wasn't long before one of Dad's old hits from the eighties blasted through the speakers. Ollie appeared and swept Cat off to dance, then of course, Mac took off with Becca.

'You OK?' asked Squidge, who by now had his video camera out ready to film the proceedings.

Squidge wants to be a film director when he leaves school and, ever since I've known him, I've never seen him without his camera. He takes it everywhere and has a wall full of recorded material in his bedroom. Mum asked him to film our Christmas party last year and she was so pleased with the results that she asked if he'd do this one as well.

I nodded. 'Yeah, sure. You go ahead and start your filming.'

After Squidge had gone, I sat at one of the tables and picked at some grapes. It looked like everyone was having a great time. Cat with Ollie, Mac with Becca, Mum with

Dad, Michael and Usha, and Star, who was down from London with some new man. I felt like a spare part sitting there with no one to dance with, but it wasn't long before Dad spotted me and hauled me up on to the floor. After a few numbers, he had to go and greet some friends who had just arrived, so I sat down again. I was hoping Star would come and say 'Hi', but she looked too busy with her new boyfriend. Like Ollie, she's never short of admirers. I guess I'm the odd one out in our family, in fact Dad even has a joke about it. He calls me the white sheep because, in comparison to the rest of them, I'm quiet whereas they're all outgoing and mega-confident. Sometimes I think I must be a disappointment to them. They're all so sociable and popular. Ollie with the girls, Star with the boys and of course Dad, with his enormous fan club. And then me. It's not that I'm *not* sociable, it's just that I'm shyer than they are – until I get to know someone. That's part of the reason I liked hanging around in a large group at my old school. There were so many of us that people didn't notice that I was quieter than the rest.

I was just starting to feel self-conscious sitting there on my own, when I spied Seth and Charlie from school. At least they'd be someone to talk to, I thought. I was about to go over when someone tapped me on the shoulder. It was one of the magicians Mum had hired to circulate amongst the guests and do magic tricks. He was wearing a half mask and a cloak and produced a five pound note and a cigarette from his sleeve. He held up the note, lit the cigarette, then burned a hole in the money with the cigarette, only when I looked at the fiver, there was no trace of a hole. It was amazing.

'How did you do that?' I gasped. I *saw* him burn the hole in the fiver and I was so close, I would have seen if he'd replaced the note with another.

He grinned. 'Magic.'

Just at that moment, someone else in a full mask and cloak tapped him on the shoulder and said something. The first magician nodded and moved away.

'So, want to see another trick?' asked the man. I nodded. He got out a five pound note and a cigarette, then lit the cigarette.

'Er, your friend has just done that trick,' I said.

Too late. The magician was pushing the cigarette through the fiver, but this time, it didn't go through. It set the fiver on fire!

'Oh *no*,' he cried as he dropped the fiver on the floor and stamped on it. 'Looks easier than it is.'

I started to laugh as I recognised the voice. 'Jonno,' I said.

He peeled off his mask. 'Hi, Lia. I knew it was you under your mask. Um, Seth and Charlie said you'd invited them. They're over by the ice sculpture, in fact, I think Seth may have got his tongue stuck to it . . . Hope you don't mind me, er . . .'

'Gate-crashing?' I asked.

He looked sheepish. 'Yeah, and almost burning down the marquee.' Jonno gave me a cheeky smile. 'Er, maybe I'd better go . . .'

I glanced over at the dance floor where by now, everyone was slow dancing to one of Sting's ballads. Shall I, shan't I? I asked myself. Jonno was still looking at me as if to gauge whether I minded him being there. He was very attractive in a Keanu Reeves kind of way . . . Oh, why not? I thought. Kaylie's not here. Jonno is very cute, why shouldn't I enjoy myself with him? I got up, took his hand and led him to the dance floor. He pulled me close and put his arms around my waist.

'Bit different here to the school disco.' He smiled, then leaned in and kissed me gently on the lips. 'Happy Valentine's Day,' he whispered in my ear.

Over his shoulder, I could see Becca. She was standing with Mac and Charlie who were trying to separate Seth from the ice sculpture. She looked over at me and gave me the thumbs-up.

Picked On

5

IT WAS the following Monday at school that it all started.

I was in the corridor on my way to the art class and Kaylie was coming the other way with Fran. She was walking towards class and she steered off course and straight into me causing me to drop my books.

'Oh, *so* sorry, Ophelia,' she said with a fake smile. 'Wasn't looking where I was going.'

'S'OK,' I said as I picked up my things. 'And please call me Lia. No one calls me Ophelia.'

My parents christened me Ophelia Moonbeam. How naff is that? I never use that name as everyone calls me Lia and I certainly never tell anyone, but it was read out on the first day of registration last autumn. I didn't think anyone had taken much notice. Amazingly, Kaylie seemed to have remembered.

'But it *is* your name, isn't it?' insisted Kaylie.

'Yeah, but . . .' I started, then I decided to confront what I thought was probably really bothering her. 'Look, about Jonno. I didn't mean for anything to happen. He just kind of . . .'

'Yeah, yeah . . .'

'He came after me.'

'That's not what I saw. You were all over him at the school disco.'

'I *wasn't*. He came over to *me*. In fact, I purposely tried to stay out of his way, because I knew you liked him.'

'Yeah, so that's why you were snogging him later at your parent's do.' said Kaylie with a toss of her hair. 'Anyway, it's his loss.'

'Well, I just wanted you to know that I didn't set out to get him.'

'Yeah, right. That's not what I heard. Oh, don't worry, everyone knows you begged him to go to your party.'

'I didn't,' I said. 'He just turned up.'

'That's not what Seth said.'

'Seth? I did invite him and Charlie, but Jonno came along with them.'

Kaylie put a finger under her chin and feigned surprise. 'Oh and *what* a coincidence that they just happen to be Jonno's mates from the football team.'

'Honestly Kaylie, he just turned up.'

'Whatever,' said Kaylie again. 'That's your story. But

then we all know about you and your stories, don't we?'

'What do you mean?'

Kaylie shrugged and made a face at Fran. 'Why you had to leave your old school.'

'I don't know what you're talking about. What are you saying?'

Kaylie smiled one of her fake smiles. 'Oh, nothing, Lia. Come *on*, we're just teasing you. Lighten up. Honestly, you're like . . . *so* intense.' She put her hand on my shoulder and gave me a gentle shove. 'Don't take things so seriously.'

And with that, she flounced into class. I felt close to tears. And confused. Was I being oversensitive? Taking it all too seriously? It felt like she'd had a real go at me, but it was done with such a smile that I couldn't be sure. Maybe I was imagining things.

'Hey, Lia, everything all right?' asked a voice behind me.

I turned. It was Squidge.

'So what was all that about?' he asked. 'I saw Kaylie walk into you. What's her problem?'

'Bad loser, I guess. I don't think she's too happy about the fact that I got off with Jonno and she didn't.'

Squidge raised his eyes to the ceiling. 'Sour grapes, huh? Well, you take no notice of her and if she gives you any trouble, you let me know, OK?'

I nodded.

'So,' continued Squidge, 'you and Jonno? You going out with him now?'

I grinned. 'Well, it's still early days, but . . . so far, so good. We've got a proper date on Saturday. Going out somewhere, don't know where yet.'

Squidge looked at me with concern for a moment, then turned to go. 'Better get to class,' he said. 'Hope it all works out for you, Lia. You deserve a decent bloke, someone who really appreciates you. Don't let any stupid girl ruin it all for you.'

'Thanks, Squidge. You're a mate.'

As he took off down the corridor I took a deep breath and followed Kaylie and Fran into class. I hoped that they weren't going to make an issue of me going out with Jonno. It wasn't my fault that he'd chosen me and not Kaylie. And I didn't have any regrets. I'd had a great time with him at the party and we even saw each other again on Sunday. He came up to the house after breakfast and we talked for hours – about school and what music we like and what we want to do after we finish school. He wants to get into the music business, so he asked me loads of questions about what it was like having a rock star dad. He stayed and had lunch with us and was well impressed by Dad's gold records. Dad even showed him around his studio and that's not something he does with many people. I think he realised that Jonno was serious about pursuing music as a career. I really like him. He was clearly starstruck by Dad, but he still paid me loads of attention and seemed genuinely interested in what I was into.

No, stuff you, Kaylie O'Hara, I thought as I took my place at a table with Cat and Becca. I'm not going to let you run my life.

The next class was English and I made sure that I was out of the art room first and along the corridor so that Kaylie and the Clones couldn't 'accidentally' bump into me again.

'You're in a hurry,' said Cat catching up with me. 'What's the rush?'

'Oh nothing,' I said. 'Just wanted to go through some notes before the lesson starts.'

Cat gave me a look like she didn't quite believe me, but she let it go. I didn't want to tell her about the run in with Kaylie before art, because I hoped it would all blow over. If I told Cat and Becca about it, they'd take my side and stick up for me and maybe start something. No best ignore it, I thought, and it will all go away.

'Right,' said Mrs Ashton, our English teacher, once we'd all taken our places. 'First, I'll give you your essays back, then I thought we'd have a quick quiz to see who's remembered what from this term.' She began to walk up and down the aisles, putting people's work in front of them on their desks. 'Well done,' she said when she got to me.

Cat caught my eye and grinned, but behind her, I saw

Kaylie whisper something to Susie Cooke and they both looked over at me and giggled.

When she'd handed out the essays, Mrs Ashton went back to her desk. 'Some of the work has been to a very high standard and I was impressed,' she said. 'George Gaynor, well done. Sunita Ahmed, also good. Lia Axford, excellent. Nick Thorn, keep up the good work. Becca Howard, an improvement. I'm glad to see you're putting your mind to your work at last.' Then she paused. 'Sadly, there were a number of essays that . . . how can I put it . . . ? Needed work, would be being polite. What has happened to some of you lately? I won't mention names, but you know who you are by your low grades and I'll be keeping an eye on you for the rest of the term.' She gave Kaylie and the Clones a pointed look, but Kaylie just raised an eyebrow and looked away.

Mrs Ashton adjusted her glasses and began to read from a sheet of paper in front of her. 'OK. Question one. Finish this sentence: King Solomon had three hundred wives and seven hundred what . . . ? Frances Wilton, maybe you'd like to stop staring out of the window and give us the answer?'

'Um . . . seven hundred porcupines, Miss.'

The class cracked up laughing.

'OK, what did she mean to say?' asked Mrs Ashton looking around.

Laura Johnson raised her hand. 'Concubines,' she said.

Mrs Ashton looked over at Fran. 'Exactly. What on earth would Solomon have done with hundreds of porcupines?'

Frances went bright red and looked at her desk as Mrs Ashton went on to the next question. 'Caesar was murdered on the Ides of March. His last words were . . .'

Mark Keegan stuck his hand up this time.

'Yes, Mark,' said Mrs Ashton.

'Tee hee, Brutus,' said Mark.

Once again, the class started laughing and Mark smiled broadly, pleased that his answer had got a laugh.

'I get the impression that you're not taking this quiz seriously, Mark,' said Mrs Ashton, then she looked around. 'The attitude of some of the people in this class will have to change or else it will show on your end of term reports. So. Anyone like to tell me what Caesar's last words really were?'

She looked around the class. I knew the answer, but I didn't want to be a Norma Know-It-All. However, Mrs Ashton looked over at me. 'Lia?'

'Um, *et tu* Brute,' I muttered.

'Correct. Without the "um", though. Well done, Lia.'

Kaylie looked over at Fran Wilton and raised her eyebrows. I should have said I didn't know, I thought. Now they will think I'm a swotty nerd.

'Now,' said Mrs Ashton, going back to her quiz. 'Kaylie O'Hara. Here's one for you. Shakespeare . . .' She adjusted her glasses and began to read. 'When was William Shakespeare born?'

'On his birthday,' said Kaylie as if it was absolutely obvious.

Once again, the class cracked up and I glanced over at Kaylie and noticed that she was blushing slightly. Unlike Mark who had given his answer for a laugh, I got the feeling that Kaylie thought that she'd given the right answer.

'Of *course* he was born on his *birth*day, Kaylie,' said Mrs Ashton. 'Anybody like to give me the actual year?'

Joss Peters put his hand up. '1564,' he said.

'Correct,' said Mrs Ashton, who then turned back to Kaylie. 'OK, Kaylie. Here's an easy one for you. We've been doing *Romeo and Juliet* this term. What was Romeo's last wish?'

'To be laid by Juliet,' said Kaylie.

This got a huge laugh especially from the boys. Kaylie looked over at me with a hard expression in her eyes, as though daring me to join in the laughter. I kept my face straight.

'I think what you meant to say was that Romeo's last wish was to die alongside Juliet, Kaylie. Like Frances, try and pay more attention to how you express yourself.'

Kaylie nodded and looked bored. 'Yes, Miss,' she drawled.

'And now for the last question,' said Mrs Ashton. 'Jackie Reeves, I think you can have this one.'

Kaylie looked over at her mate and sighed as though Mrs Ashton's comments were all a great waste of time.

'The most famous composer in the world is?' asked Mrs Ashton.

'Um . . . Bach. Um . . . Handel,' drawled Jackie.

There was a snigger from the back of the class as Mrs Ashton sighed. 'Anyone like to tell us what's wrong with that?' she asked.

This time I kept my head down. Luckily, Sunita Ahmed put her hand up. 'It's got to be either one or the other, Miss. Either Bach is the most famous or Handel. Not both.'

Jackie gave Sunita a really filthy look and I could see that, like me, Sunita suddenly felt as though she wished she'd kept her mouth shut.

'Exactly,' said Mrs Ashton with a weary sigh. 'But I've heard worse. One pupil once told me that Handel was half German, half Italian and half English . . . Anyone like to comment?'

A few people tittered, but no one spoke. 'Come on class, it's not difficult. Wake up. Who can tell me what's wrong with that? Cat Kennedy?'

'Um, the maths aren't quite right. If he was half German, half Italian and half English, he'd be one and a half people.'

'Correct,' said Mrs Ashton. 'Now all of you, I don't want

to see any of you making these types of mistakes, not in my class. It shows you're not thinking. We have pupils like George, Sunita, Nick and Lia in the class setting a standard. Try and learn from them.'

The Clones all started sniggering at this and Mrs Ashton saw them. 'Seeing as you find the whole thing so amusing, Susie Cooke, you can answer the next question. Who was it Salome danced naked in front of?'

Susie shrugged her shoulders like she didn't care.

'Come on, Susie,' said Mrs Ashton. 'We only did it last week.'

I could see Kaylie mouthing an answer to her mate. Susie screwed up her eyes to try and read Kaylie's lips then she nodded.

'Harrods,' she said.

Mrs Ashton looked up at the ceiling. 'Herod, Susie. Not *Harrods*. Harrods is a shop in Knightsbridge.'

I glanced over at Kaylie and she was staring at me again with narrowed eyes. It was hard not to laugh at what her and the Clones had said, especially as most of the class was giggling away. Becca and Cat may be right, I thought. Kaylie and her mates may be popular and trendy, but they're not very bright. I stared back at Kaylie thinking, two can play at this game and I'm not going to be intimidated by you. After a few minutes, she leaned back in her chair and whispered something to Fran behind her. Fran glanced over at me and laughed. I turned away. She wasn't worth it and I didn't want to get into playing stupid games. All I wanted was to go to school, do my lessons and get on with everyone without any aggro. Sadly, though, by the look on Kaylie's face, she wasn't going to let that happen.

6

A Turn for the Worse

THE NEXT day, I went into school determined not to let Kaylie and the Clones phase me. I'd tough it out, be all smiling and friendly. But they decided to try a new tactic. They just plain ignored me. When I saw them in the corridor before assembly, I said hi, and they all turned the other way like they'd smelled a bad smell. It was weird, I felt like I was invisible or something.

'What's up with them?' asked Becca, when she noticed them give me the cold shoulder.

'Oh nothing,' I said. 'I think Kaylie's got it in for me because of Jonno.'

'God. How pathetic,' said Becca, giving them a scornful look.

Suddenly Kaylie came bustling over and stood between Becca and me with her back to me. 'I hear you're going to be helping Miss Segal produce the end-of-year show,' she said.

'That's right,' said Becca moving to the right to include me in the conversation.

Kaylie moved, obscuring my view again. 'Do you know what it's going to be yet?'

Becca nodded. 'Nothing official, but I'm pretty sure we're going to be doing *The Rocky Horror Picture Show*.'

'Oh, top!' said Kaylie then beckoned to her mates and began to sing, 'Let's do the time warp again.'

Fran, Susie and Jackie came over to join us. '*Rocky Horror*. Excellent. Can we be in it?' asked Fran. I moved to stand with them, but Susie stepped to the left once again keeping me out of the circle.

Becca glanced at me with a worried expression. 'Casting is in the main hall on Saturday afternoon,' she said.

'Cool,' said Kaylie, then she took a step back and stood on my toes.

'Ow!' I cried.

'Oh, *sooo* sorry, Ophelia. I didn't see you there.' Then she gave me a snooty look and turned back to Becca. 'I suppose *some* people wanting a part will be taking advantage of the fact that their mate is the producer.'

'I doubt it,' said Becca. 'Best man wins, as always.'

'Good,' said Kaylie. 'Because we don't want anyone getting in for the wrong reasons or because their dad is in the music business or anything.'

'Knock it off, Kaylie,' said Becca. 'You know people get

in because of their individual performances. Who's right for the part and so on.'

'Yeah right,' said Kaylie. 'Well, we'll see shall we?'

'What's going on?' asked Becca when they'd gone. 'They were, like, totally blanking you.'

'I know,' I said. 'They were a bit weird with me yesterday as well, to be honest, but I'm not going to let it get to me.'

'Good. They're not worth it. So you'll be at the casting session, won't you? I think it will be a total gas doing *The Rocky Horror Picture Show*. Mac will do the scenery and, of course, Squidge will film it, so it will be a laugh, all of us together.'

I hesitated. I had no illusions about my singing so wouldn't expect to get a lead role, but I can dance and had hoped that maybe I could be in the chorus. Plus, Miss Segal is my favourite teacher. It's like she's really tuned in to people and can bring out the best in them. But if Kaylie was going to be there making jibes at me at every rehearsal, maybe it wouldn't be much fun.

'Not sure yet,' I said.

Becca grimaced. 'If you let them put you off, I'll . . . I'll . . .'

'You won't speak to me either,' I laughed. 'Then *no one* will be speaking to me.'

Becca linked her arm through mine. 'I'd never do that,' she said.

I decided to confide in Becca. If anyone would understand how mean girls can be, it would be her. Recently, she'd had a run-in with Mac's sister, Jade, when both of them went up for a national singing competition to find a 'Pop Princess'. Jade can be a total cow when she wants and she acted really unfriendly and unsupportive. She even tricked Becca into saying something negative on the phone about one of the competitors when, unaware to Becca, the girl was listening in on an extension.

'Only reason I'm hesitating is that . . .' I started. 'Look, I know people gossip about my dad and our house and stuff locally, but I don't want that to affect things here at school. I just want to be normal. To fit in with everyone else and for now, until Kaylie's got over whatever's bugging her, that's more important than having a role in the school show. Do you understand?'

Becca nodded, then shook her head. 'I do, but don't let them walk all over you. I've seen them do it to girls in our year before. You have to stand up to them. Don't let them win. They don't bother me, I can tell you that. Do you want me to have a word with them?'

'*No*,' I said. '*Please*. That would only make an issue of it, and they'll get all sniffy about me talking to you about them. No. Please, don't get into it. Let me sort it my way, OK?'

'OK,' said Becca. 'But you know that whatever they do, I'm on your side. Right?'

'Right,' I said.

On my side, she said. Though I appreciated the support, I felt sad. Already, it was about taking sides. Oh, why can't I just fit in? Have my mates and not be noticed? All I want is to be accepted.

In the changing rooms on Wednesday, things took a turn for the worse. The Clones all stood in one corner and were whispering and looking at me as I was getting changed for gym. It was awful. Everyone seems to have got boobs except me. I've shot up to five-foot-seven, yet still have the shape of a nine-year-old boy. Becca's really sweet about it. She says I'm the perfect shape to be a model and she wishes she was like me, but I think she's just being kind. I wish I was more like her. She's got a great figure – really curvy, although she thinks she's fat. I guess no one's ever happy with their body. Even Cat, who is perfect, thinks she's too short.

As the Clones continued staring, I began to think I'd grown an extra breast or something. Then I remembered what Becca had said about standing up to them so I turned around and asked, 'What are you looking at?'

Of course, they all turned away and looked at the floor or the wall – except Kaylie, that is. She leaned on her right hip, stuck her chin out at me and said, 'Think a lot of yourself, don't you?'

'No,' I replied. 'What do you mean?'

'Like, *why* would we be staring at you? You've a problem you know, Lia. You think everything is about you when it isn't. People do have their own lives you know.'

I didn't know what to say, so I looked away. I felt confused again. They *had* been staring at me, I'm sure of it, but Kaylie had managed to turn everything around and make out that it was me who had the problem. Maybe she was right. Maybe I *am* getting obsessive about them. I had certainly spent a lot of time thinking about them and how to handle them over the past few days. Maybe I do spend too much time thinking about myself and what people think of me. Maybe it *is* me. Maybe I do have a problem.

As the week went on, I tried to tell myself that it didn't matter, but by Thursday, I felt more confused than ever and I dreaded going into school for fear of what they were going to do or say.

I've always been happy enough at school, but suddenly, it felt like some ordeal I had to endure. All I wanted was just to get to the end of the day so that I could go home. I tried my best to stay out of their way, but it's hard when we have so many classes together. I was sure I wasn't imagining it. Every time I saw the Clones, it seemed like they'd been busy chatting to people, but as soon as I arrived, everyone would go quiet for a moment in a guilty sort of way and sometimes they'd laugh. I wondered what they were saying about me, but I daren't ask for fear that Kaylie would tell me that I was self-obsessed again and that people had other things to talk about besides Lia Axford.

Friday was the final straw. At break, I met up with Cat and Becca and both of them were holding little pink invitations cards.

'Invite to Kaylie's tomorrow night,' said Becca. 'Shall we go after the casting session?'

'Dunno,' said Cat. 'I mean, those girls aren't exactly our best mates and she's never asked us before.'

'All the more reason to go and see what it's like,' said Becca. 'I bet loads of people will be going and there's nothing else happening.'

'I think that may be another reason that Kaylie is jealous of you, Lia,' said Cat. 'Before your family arrived, the do's at Kaylie's house were legendary. I think your mum's parties have stolen her thunder a bit.'

'Understatement,' said Becca. 'I bet she's seething, mainly because you've never invited her. In fact, she's probably jealous of every aspect of your life. A glam rock star dad, an ex-model mum, a fab mansion to live in, latest clothes . . .'

'Gorgeous brother, gorgeous sister . . .' said Cat. 'The list is endless.'

'But it's not my fault,' I said. 'I didn't choose my parents or my family . . .'

'Yeah, but she would have, given half the chance,' said Becca. 'And she hasn't even got a look-in to any part of it.'

'How come she holds so many parties?' I asked.

'Partly because she likes to be popular and being "hostess with the mostest" gives her a chance to surround herself with people,' said Becca. 'Plus, her mum works night shifts in a hospital over in Plymouth, so she has a free reign of her house most evenings.'

'What about her dad?' I asked. 'Surely he's home.'

Cat shook her head. 'Disappeared years ago. Rumour has it he ran off with the barmaid from the Crown and Anchor. Anyway, it's an empty house at the weekend and where else is there for teenagers to go round here in the winter? Weekends, a lot of people hang out at Kaylie's.'

'I wonder if her mum knows that she uses the house,' I said.

'Doubt it,' said Becca. 'She probably gets her little clones to tidy up for her afterwards. So shall we go? It might be a laugh if we all go together. What do you think, Lia. You up for it?'

'She hasn't invited me,' I said.

'Are you sure?' asked Becca. 'Why would she invite us and not you? Look again. I saw her putting cards on everyone's desk. Maybe yours fell off, go back and look.'

I didn't have to. Not after the week I'd had. I had a feeling that she'd excluded me on purpose. It was weird, because she hadn't done anything major, not like when a boy bullies another boy. That might be simpler to deal with, I thought. If someone kicks or smacks you about, there's no doubt about it – you're being bullied. But this? I wasn't sure what was going on and wondered if it was all in my imagination. What had been happening was so subtle. Almost unseen. Secret looks between Kaylie and her mates, or whispers or sniggers, and now, no invite to her party. Plus, I felt there was no way I could go to the casting session. No big deal, not really. But inside, I felt like Kaylie had got it in for me and I felt miserable.

First Date

7

'PENNY FOR them,' said Dad, making me jump as he came up behind me.

'Oh, sorry, I was miles away.'

It was Saturday morning and I was sitting in the kitchen, gazing out of the window and going over the week in my mind.

'I could see that,' said Dad. 'So what's going on in that head of yours? How's your week been?'

'Oh . . . fine.'

'Hmm. You sure? You don't look your usual bright self and you've been quieter than usual this week.'

'No, honest. I'm great.'

'Everything OK at school?'

'Yeah.'

'Everything OK with Jonno?'

'Yeah, in fact, he's coming up tonight. We're going out somewhere.'

55

'You don't sound too excited. Tonight's a first date, isn't it?'

I nodded. He was right. I wasn't too excited. It was as if, in putting up a wall in my head to keep Kaylie out, I'd kept everything else out as well.

'So what is it, pet?' asked Dad. 'Come on, spill. You don't live in the same house as someone and not notice when something's going on.'

'Honest, Dad. It's nothing. Just . . . do you think I'm self-obsessed?'

Dad laughed. 'What kind of question is that? What do you mean?'

'You know, always thinking about myself?'

Dad laughed again. 'All teenagers are self-obsessed. It's part of the package. And, to a degree, so is everyone else. I mean, you live in your body, in your world. You're the only one who sees things through your eyes, so you're bound to be a little self-obsessed.'

I laughed.

'Maybe we need another word,' said Dad. 'Not "obsessed" . . . um, self-motivated. That sounds better, more positive. But why did you ask that, Lia? Is something worrying you?'

I sighed and tried to decide how much to tell him. Sometimes if you get parents involved, they worry. Then they end up becoming more of a problem than the problem itself. I decided to tell him part of the story.

'It's like . . . well, there's this girl and her mates at school, and I don't think they like me very much. I haven't ever done anything bad to them, but they seem to have it in for me.'

Dad pulled up a stool, took my hand and looked me directly in the eye. 'Are you being bullied, Lia?'

'*No*. No. That's exactly it. I'm not. But it almost feels like I am. But then, I don't know if it's me being paranoid or self-obsessed. Thinking too much about what other people think of me, when they're not even thinking about me at all . . . Oh, I don't know. It's OK, Dad, really. I know I'm not even making any sense. It's just, I want to fit in. You know, new school. But it's like some people won't even give me a chance.'

'Could be they're jealous,' said Dad, indicating our vast, top-of-the-range kitchen with his hand. 'We do live very well compared to most. And, you are a very pretty girl . . .'

'Yeah, yeah . . .'

'Seriously. It could be that.'

'I don't think these girls are jealous. I'm not sure. I mean, one of them was a bit miffed that I got off with Jonno, but these girls are popular and very pretty. The Teen Queens. It's not like I'm any kind of threat to their position in the school.'

Dad nodded. 'Yes, but you got Jonno and they didn't. They might think, first you get him, what's next?'

'Nothing. I just want to be ordinary.'

'Then sorry, Lia, can't help you. You'll never be ordinary, not with your looks and personality. And you're a clever girl. So you'll always do well at school if you keep working. And our life, well, no one can ever say that that's ordinary, can they? Sometimes you just have to accept your lot and get on with it.'

'I know. Sorry. I'm going on about nothing. And I may be imagining it all anyway.'

'So these girls who are giving you a hard time . . . How, exactly? Calling you names? What?'

My brain felt numb for a moment as I tried to think about it. There wasn't actually anything I could say that sounded so bad. So someone stared at me and didn't say hi back. Big deal. It sounds so pathetic.

'I'm pretty sure that they're all talking about me, but not in a nice way. Sometimes they ignore me, but sometimes, like when I go into a class, everyone shuts up like they've been talking about me . . . that sort of thing.'

Dad got up to fill the coffee grinder with beans. 'What do Cat and Becca think?'

'Becca says stand up to them and I haven't really talked to Cat about it much. To tell the truth, I don't want them to get into it. You know, they might feel that they have to take sides and all that . . . I just want it all to go away.'

Dad came over and squeezed my shoulder. 'I know just how you feel, love.'

'You do? How can you? Did someone give you a hard time at school?'

'Bully me? No way. I'd have thumped anyone back who tried. But it's different with lads. If someone's a bully and tries to kick your head in, it's pretty clear what's happening. No. It was later when I first began to make a name for myself in the music business that I got bullied, but in a different kind of way to what goes on in schools.'

'Who by?'

Dad went to the fridge and got some milk. 'The press,' he said with a grim expression. 'First, they're all, Oh, the new golden boy, and they can't get enough of you. But they can turn, and when they do, boy, do you feel it! I tell you, Lia, the press can be the biggest bullies of all and they can make or break someone.'

'So what happened?'

'I was on tour in the States and there was some story about a girl I was supposed to be having an affair with. All nonsense. I sat next to her in a club and the next day it was all over the papers over here. Course, your mum got to hear about it and was livid. Didn't know what or who to believe. The more I defended my position, the more guilty I looked. I had to learn fast, believe me. No, the best way to deal with them, or those girls at your school, is not to waste any

59

energy on them. Don't rise to the challenge. Don't engage. Don't try to defend yourself as sometimes you can't win.'

'So what can you do?'

'Decide who's important in your life and be honest with them. Keep them close. But keep them out of it – gossip, rumour mongering, all of it. I've learned to keep my head down where the press are involved. But at the time, when I was younger, I used to get so mad at some of the things they'd write. Total fiction, but I had sleepless nights, thinking, What will people think? I must put the story straight, and so on. Dignified silence, that's the best. Now, I know who I can count on and they're the people who matter. They know the score and the rest of them can go to hell and believe what they want. Fame is fickle. The press are fickle. Sounds like these girls at your school are fickle. It sounds like you wouldn't want them as friends anyway, would you?'

I shook my head.

'So, there's your answer. Don't waste your energy letting them bother you. Enjoy your date tonight. And you have some great mates that care about you and they're the ones who matter. There will always be other people who won't like you, no matter what you do. Don't even give them the time of day. OK, pal?'

'OK,' I said.

'So how's about one of my cappuccino specials with extra chocolate on top?'

'Sure,' I said. I felt a lot better after talking to Dad. He was right. I'd been stupid letting it all get to me so much. In future, Kaylie and the Clones could do what they liked. I had my friends and my family, and they're the ones that counted. 'Thanks, Dad.'

Later, I went upstairs to have a bath and get ready for my date. I was really looking forward to it and wondered where Jonno would suggest going. There weren't that many places open nearby apart from pubs, so maybe he planned on going into Plymouth. I decided to make a real effort and spent ages trying on different outfits and doing my make-up. My first proper date since London. I couldn't wait.

Jonno arrived at seven o'clock, full of gossip about the casting session for *The Rocky Horror Picture Show* that had taken place at school in the afternoon.

'Did you get it?' I asked as I took him into the red sitting room. He'd played Danny Zucko in *Grease* in the Christmas show, so everyone was expecting that he'd play the lead again.

He shook his head and flopped on to a sofa. 'No, the role of Dr Frank N Furter went to Adam Hall.'

'Do you mind?'

'Nah. I'm cool with it. It can be a bit time-consuming playing the lead, and actually, I could do with some time to concentrate on other things.'

'So who got the other parts?'

'Do you know the story?'

'Vaguely. Some kids end up in a castle with a load of weirdos.'

Jonno laughed. 'That's about the gist of it. Dan Archer is playing Brad Majors and Jessica Moon is playing Janet. They're the geeky kids whose car breaks down and who end up at Frank N Furter's castle. Ryan Nolan is Riff Raff, the hunchback henchman, and Jade Macey is playing his sister, Magenta.'

'What about Cat?'

'I think she's playing the tap dancing groupie, Columbia. But where were you? I thought you'd be there.'

'Um, I decided to give it a miss this time. As you said, being in a show can be a bit full on. Did Kaylie and her mates get parts?'

Jonno nodded. 'Chorus, I think. Good job, because I doubt if they'd be able to remember their lines if they got bigger parts. They're not exactly the brightest coins in the collection, are they? Once when I was asked to coach the netball team, I said I wanted to discuss tactics. One of them, I think it was Jackie, thought I was talking about mints.'

I laughed, but wasn't quite sure if he was just joking.

'By the way, did you get the invite to Kaylie's?' he asked.

I shook my head. I hadn't thought of her party as an

option and hoped that Jonno hadn't planned on taking me there. 'No. But . . . but you go if you want.'

'No thanks,' he said getting up and going over to look at a painting on the wall opposite. 'Nice painting. Picasso, isn't it? My mum's got the same print.'

'Er, yeah, Picasso.' I didn't tell him that ours was the original, in case he thought I was showing off.

'Nah,' he continued, 'Kaylie's do's are not my scene. I find her crowd a bit too . . .' he mimicked a girlie-girl walking on high heels and flicking her hair. 'You know, lipstick, handbags and pointy shoes – that's all they think about.'

Yeah, I thought and how to ruin my life. 'So what shall we do this evening?' I asked.

Jonno came and sat next to me and took my hand. 'Ah well. I wanted to talk to you about this . . .'

At that moment, Dad came in. 'Watcha, Jonno,' he said as he turned on the television. 'Don't mind me.'

Jonno glanced at me, then looked longingly at the telly. 'Er, how about we stay here? Hang out. It's raining outside and I missed this afternoon's game . . . because of the casting session . . . and now, well, there's the . . .'

'Highlights of the Arsenal versus Man United game,' said Dad, rubbing his hands together, then bouncing on to the sofa.

***

Fifteen minutes later, Dad and Jonno were ensconced, shoes off, feet up, Cokes in hand, watching the football.

'*Woah,*' cried Dad as both of them rose in unison from the sofa when there was a near miss goal. As they settled back down again, Dad turned to look at me with one of his cheeky grins. 'Think we need another after that,' he said pointing at his Coke can.

This wasn't quite my romantic fantasy, I thought as I got up to go to the kitchen for fresh supplies. Mum was in the kitchen feeding the dogs when I went over to the fridge.

She smiled up at me. 'Not going out?'

'Arsenal versus Man United,' I said. 'I think Dad and Jonno have just discovered that they're soulmates.'

'Ah,' sighed Mum. 'Some things you just can't compete with.'

'Why did Dad have to watch in the red room? There's five other televisions in the house.'

'But that's where the biggest telly is. He got it specially for the footie. Digital sound, wide screen . . . he says he feels like he's actually there.'

'I just don't get it,' I said. 'How men can get so excited about kicking a bit of leather around a field.'

'Welcome to the club,' said Mum. 'Want to hear a joke about football?'

I nodded.

'What's the similarity between a boy and a football player?' she asked.

'Dunno.'

'They both dribble when they're trying to score.'

I laughed, then turned my head towards the door. I could hear singing. It sounded like the 'I–I–yippee, song'. Mum laughed. 'Better get used to it. Men tend to behave like kids when their beloved football's on. It can get very emotional.'

We went and stood in the hall by the red room door and, sure enough, they were both singing their hearts out. 'We're the best behaved supporters in the land, we're the best behaved supporters in the land, the best behaved supporters, best behaved supporters, the best behaved supporters in the land . . . when we win. We're a right bunch of bastards when we lose, we're a right bunch of bastards when we lose, we're a right bunch of bastards, right bunch of bastards, right bunch of bastards when we lose.'

'Hmm,' said Mum. 'Fancy a game of backgammon in the library?'

'Anything to get away from this,' I laughed, putting my hands over my ears.

I spent the evening in the library with Mum while Jonno bonded with my dad in the red room. At one point, I crept in to catch up, but they were deeply absorbed in conversation, analysing the game so far. As the second half of their programme started up, they burst into song again. This time it was to the tune of 'Glory, Glory Hallelujah'. 'Glory, Glory, Man United. Glory, Glory, Man United,' they sang. 'Glory, Glory, Man United. When the Reds keep marching on, on, on.'

'Ah, the famous rock star and the aspiring music student,' I teased from the door. 'I wish your fans could see you now, Dad.'

'I've had a *top* time,' said Jonno later when I saw him to the door. 'We must do it again soon.'

'Yeah, right,' I said as he leaned in to kiss me goodnight.

'Next week for Man United and Liverpool,' called Dad as he went up the stairs.

'Absolutely,' said Jonno, giving Dad a wave. Somehow the moment for snogging had been ruined, so I stepped back inside. Jonno didn't even seem to have noticed and went off smiling.

So much for my first date, I thought later as I wiped off my make-up.

Junk Mail?

8

THE FOLLOWING week at school, to my relief, the Clones seemed to have lost interest in me and life got back to normal. Sort of. At home, some rather strange things were starting to happen.

On Monday, when I got back from school, I had post. A catalogue advertising Tea Tree oil products for people who suffer from bad perspiration and BO. I didn't think anything of it, as so much junk mail comes through the door, so I chucked it in the bin.

Tuesday, I got a catalogue about padded bras for women who had flat chests. Quite useful, I thought, seeing as I'm as flat as a pancake. Again, I didn't think anything of it, only that our address must have gone on some mailing list somewhere. Although it was strange that it was addressed to me, as I wasn't the home owner.

Wednesday, a catalogue came for me from a company

67

selling gravestones. It couldn't be Kaylie, could it, I wondered? Surely she wouldn't go to all the trouble of getting these things sent to me? A shiver went down my spine when I thought over the things that had been sent. A catalogue for people with BO, a catalogue for padded bras and now one for gravestones. The insinuations were horrible. That I smelled, had no chest and soon might need a gravestone. No, *no*, I told myself, *no one* would be that horrible.

By the time the evening came, I had to believe that my earlier suspicions about Kaylie were right. At eight o'clock, two nettuna cheese pizzas arrived for me and I definitely hadn't ordered them. The delivery boy insisted that I had – he had my name, phone number and everything. Mum phoned the restaurant and, sure enough, they had all my details. She paid the boy, then turned to me in the hall.

'What's going on, Lia? Were you still hungry after supper and didn't want to say?'

'No. Course not. I'd tell you if I wanted pizza, you know that.'

'So who ordered these if you didn't?'

Kaylie O'Hara and her mates, I thought. And I'm pretty sure that they arranged for the catalogues to be sent as well. Mum saw me hesitate.

'Do you think you might know who ordered these?' she asked.

'Maybe . . .'

'Come on, let's go and sit down and try and get to the bottom of this.'

I followed Mum into the red room and we sat on the sofa. My mind was whirring round and round like a washing machine on spin. What to say? I couldn't be sure it was Kaylie. It might just be a mistake on the computer at the pizza restaurant. There was only one locally and we had ordered from there before, so I know they had our details on record. It was possible that they'd made a mistake. But a nagging feeling told me otherwise, although I couldn't prove anything. I felt miserable. If Kaylie was doing these things, she was doing them in a way that didn't obviously point the finger back at her. It could be her being vindictive, but it also could be me being paranoid and imagining things.

'So?' asked Mum.

'I'm not sure,' I said. 'Just at school lately, this girl has kind of got it in for me. I thought she'd dropped it as she's been pretty cool this week. Sort of back to normal, but maybe not.'

Mum nodded. 'Your dad did mention that someone had upset you. You do know that you can come to either of us don't you?'

I nodded. 'Yeah. I . . . I didn't want to make a big deal out of it.'

'Has anything else arrived out of the ordinary, Lia? I

noticed that there's been a lot of post for you this week.'

'Catalogues,' I admitted. 'At first I thought they were junk mail, but now . . .'

'What sort of catalogues?'

'One for people with BO, one for people with flat chests and one for gravestones.'

'Oh, Lia,' gasped Mum. 'Why didn't you say anything?'

'Because I'm not a hundred per cent sure, you know how much rubbish comes through the door – people advertising everything from windows to life insurance.'

'Yes, but all that stuff comes to me or your father. There's no reason why mail order firms would have your name. If it *is* this girl, then she has to be stopped. Do you want me to have a word with your class teacher?'

'*No!*' I cried. 'God *no*, that would be the worst thing ever. What if it wasn't her? Maybe it's just coincidence. She's already accused me of being self-obsessed . . .'

'One coincidence I could buy,' said Mum softly, 'but not this many.'

The thought of Mum going into the school filled me with horror. I imagined the teachers ticking Kaylie off, then she'd spread it around that I'd ratted on her, then there'd be even more talking about me behind my back and sniggering behind hands. No, Mum mustn't go in. I decided to try and make light of the situation.

'It's not a big deal, Mum. Not really. I thought it would

all blow over and maybe it has. But if it *was* Kaylie who ordered the pizzas and you went and talked to the teachers, then I'd be labelled as a sneak.'

'But Lia darling, you can't let her get away with this.'

'I know.'

'So what do you want to do?'

'Don't know,' I sighed. 'I really don't know.'

'Do I know this girl?' asked Mum, putting her arm around me.

I shook my head. 'Doubt it.'

'What's her name?'

'Kaylie. But please, Mum, don't do anything about it. I can handle it.'

'Well, you'll keep me informed as to what's going on, won't you?'

'Sure,' I said. It was good to know I had her support, but another part of me felt like I was letting her down. Star was so popular at school and Ollie is at his. And it's not that I wasn't popular. Lots of people thought I was OK, but I knew that could change if Kaylie carried on poisoning people's minds about me. Already, I was noticing that people in our class weren't being quite as friendly as they had been. God, I hate this, I thought. I really, really hate it. Why can't Kaylie just leave me alone? Heaven knows what people are thinking.

I had to make sure that Mum didn't make things worse.

'I'll talk to her. Please, Mum, let me deal with it.'

The next morning before school, Meena called me down into the hall. She was holding a huge bunch of tulips.

'Who are they for?' I asked.

'For you. See, here your name. No message, though.'

Oh, not Kaylie again, I thought, but then she wouldn't send me flowers. Must be from Jonno, I decided as I took the bouquet. How sweet. He must have felt bad about neglecting me Saturday. I went to phone him immediately.

'But . . . but they're not from me,' he said. 'Sorry. Should be, I suppose, I just didn't think of it. Looks like you have another admirer. Hmm . . . don't know if I like that. No message, you say?'

'Not an admirer,' I said. 'I think I might know who sent them and believe me, you've got no competition. Er, see you at school later.'

Just as I was about to leave for school, Mum called me into her room. 'I've just had a call from the florists, Lia. They say that you called yesterday and ordered some flowers. They called to ask if I wanted to change my usual weekly order of white lilies to tulips from now on.'

I shook my head. 'Sorry, Mum. I think it might be Kaylie stirring it again.'

Mum sighed. 'Darling, we have to do something.'

'I know, I know,' I said. I could kill Kaylie, I thought. But then that's probably just what she wanted – a confrontation so that she can deny everything and make me look like a fool. But now this was getting out of hand. She was involving Mum. I wondered what else she'd ordered in my name that Mum would have to pay for.

When I got to school, Kaylie, Jackie, Susie and Fran were all standing in their usual spot near the radiators in the hall. I saw them look over when I walked in and Kaylie said something and they all giggled.

How to play it, I thought. I guess they're waiting for me to be upset or mad. Well, I'm not going to be.

I smiled as I went by. 'Hi. Lovely day, isn't it?'

Ha. A puzzled expression flashed across Kaylie's face. She couldn't ask if I'd got the post or flowers, as that would identify her as the person sending things. And she'd never know if I got them or not if I didn't react. Yes, that was how to play it. She could deny sending me things and I could deny ever getting anything.

Sadly, though, my lack of reaction only made Kaylie react more. It was just after RE at the end of the day and most of the class had filed out. I asked Cat if I could borrow a book. 'Yeah, sure. In my bag,' she said, pointing to her rucksack. But then she suddenly tried to grab it before I did. 'Er, *no*, let me get it for you.'

I was instantly suspicious. There was something in her bag she didn't want me to see. Maybe another invite to one of Kaylie's little weekend parties. I didn't mind that, but I did mind Cat hiding stuff from me.

I looked into her bag before she could stop me and saw a piece of pink paper folded up next to the books. Kaylie always wrote on pink. I quickly pulled it out and began to read it.

'Oh no,' said Cat. '*Please* don't read that. I *so* didn't want you to see it.'

My face must have fallen, because Cat put her arm around me. 'Lia, she's not worth it. Nobody's going to believe what she's written.'

It said:

To Year Nine,
If you ever wondered why Lia Axford left her last school, this is why. She was expelled for lying and making up stories about classmates to try and make out that they were doing bad things. Be very careful what she says about anyone, as it will be lies. She twists events to make people think that everything is about her. Remember – Lia equals LIAR.

I felt tears sting my eyes. 'It's not true!' I blurted. 'I left my old school because I wanted to live at home. That's all.'

74

Cat put her arms around me. 'We know that, Lia. That's why I didn't want you to see the note.'

'*Why* has she got it in for me? I don't understand.'

'Because she's a mean, spiteful cow,' said Cat. 'And she's jealous because you've got everything that she wants.'

I glanced up and saw Susie peering through the glass pane at the classroom door. I didn't even bother to try and hide that I was crying. OK, result, I thought. You got me. Made me cry. Now go and tell your leader. Let her know Lia's in tears and I hope you'll all be very happy.

9 Negotiation Time

I DECIDED I had to take action. Put a stop to it. And there was only one way to do it. Cat had said that I had everything that Kaylie wanted, and that included Jonno. So the solution was simple.

'What do you mean you don't want to meet up later? Why?' he asked, when I saw him outside the gates after school.

'Look, it's not you, it's me . . .' I started.

'It's because I watched the game with your dad last week, isn't it? I *knew* it was a mistake. Girls always hate it when blokes watch the footie. Look, I won't do it again if you don't want me to.'

'It's not that Jonno. I didn't mind. Not really.'

'So what is it, then?'

This was proving more difficult than I'd thought. I couldn't come up with a logical reason. I did like him.

'It doesn't make sense, Lia. Come on, talk to me. We get on really well, so what's the problem?'

'Just . . . things are a bit awkward at the moment. Maybe we could go out at a later date. In a month or so?'

Jonno looked bewildered. 'Now you're really not making sense. Unless . . . is there someone else you've been seeing and you have to finish with him?'

'No. No one else.'

'So *what*, then? Come on. This is crazy.'

At that moment, Becca walked past. 'Phone me later, Lia,' she called.

'Sure,' I said.

Jonno waved her over. 'Hey, Becca. Lia doesn't want to see me any more and won't tell me why. You're her mate. Can you enlighten me?'

Becca looked surprised and glanced at me, then back at Jonno. 'Kaylie O'Horrible,' she said.

'What's she got to do with it?' asked Jonno.

Becca nudged me. 'I think you should tell him, Lia. She can't rule people's lives like this.'

'What is going on?' asked Jonno, who by now looked really confused. 'What do you mean, Kaylie can't rule people's lives?'

'She's been giving Lia a hard time,' Becca blurted out, 'because you're going out with Lia and not with her.'

Jonno narrowed his eyes and his expression turned to thunder. 'A hard time? Like how?'

'Telling lies about Lia, for a start,' said Becca. 'Spreading rumours.'

Jonno turned to face me. 'Why didn't you tell me?'

I felt at a loss to say anything. I felt so mixed up. Part of me felt relieved, as I'd been worried that he might have heard something about the note and wondered if it was true, if I really was a liar. Another part just wanted to escape from everything. It was all happening too fast. My head suddenly felt vacant, like someone had sucked all the air out of it. I saw Jonno glance behind Becca and me at a crowd coming out of school. Kaylie and the Clones were amongst them. Jonno took one look at them and went straight over.

'Oh hell, now what have you started, Becca?' I asked.

Becca looked hurt. 'Look, I told you I'm on your side. Girls like her can't be allowed to get away with it. I saw that note she sent round class. You – *we* – have to stand up to them.'

I strained to hear what Jonno was saying to Kaylie. Whatever it was, it looked heated and a small crowd gathered to see what was going on. Jonno is easily the most popular boy in school and Kaylie wouldn't like the fact that he was yelling at her in public. She was shifting about on her feet and looking at the pavement as though she wanted it to swallow her. Jonno finished what he was saying, then turned to leave. As he walked back towards us, he turned back. 'Just stay out of my business and grow up, Kaylie. I'll see who I choose and it wouldn't be you even if you were the last girl on the planet.'

'You'd be so lucky,' she called after him. But she looked upset.

Oh finking stinking, I thought as my stomach twisted into a knot. What now? I know Becca meant well. I know Jonno meant well, but now it was all out in the open, in front of the whole school. Jonno came back to me and put his arm around my shoulder. I glanced back at Kaylie as he began to lead me away and she gave me the filthiest look. If looks could kill, I thought, I'd be six foot under. It was awful. Everyone was staring and I knew it would be all around the school in half an hour. So much for fitting in and lying low, I thought. She's never going to let that happen now.

Jonno seemed to think that his 'conversation' with Kaylie had put an end to the idea of finishing with him. And quite honestly, it didn't seem to matter any more. Whether I was with Jonno or not, it was too late. Kaylie had been humiliated in public. War had been declared, and though not directly by me, I was in the front line whether I liked it or not.

Jonno and Becca stayed with me as I waited for Meena to pick me up. Only when they saw Kaylie and the Clones pile on the bus with the other school kids, did they go off on their various ways, Jonno to football practice and

Becca to a production meeting with Miss Segal.

This is ridiculous, I thought. Now they think I need bodyguards.

As Meena drove me home, I had a good long hard think. The situation couldn't continue like this. I didn't want to fight with Kaylie or any of her mates. Or argue with them. I just wanted to get on.

'What would you do if someone waged war on you, Meena?' I asked.

'Hmmm,' she said as she drove down the windy roads towards our house. 'I no like war. I think is big waste of time, money and innocent lives. Best not have war.'

'Yes, but if someone starts a war against you, even though you don't want it, what then?'

'Once I read book by Mahatma Gandhi. He leader of India for long time. He had good philosophy. He say that before resorting to war, one should always try the peaceful approach. Make effort to negotiate.'

I hadn't thought of taking that approach. I'd thought my only two options were to back off or fight. Hmm. Negotiate. Maybe I should give it a try. Plus, Mum's always saying that there's good in everyone. Kaylie must have feelings; she's only human. There's bound to be a heart in there somewhere. Maybe I could appeal to her better nature.

When I got home, I went straight to my room and

turned on my computer. I opened my Outlook Express and looked for the folder of old e-mails. There was one in particular I was looking for. It was from before Christmas, before everything went weird with Kaylie. It was one of those chain letters that tells you to send it on to ten people immediately or else something awful will happen to you. It had been sent around to just about everyone in the school and before you got to the actual message, there were about five pages of people's e-mail addresses. I vaguely remembered Kaylie's being on the list. It was blondebombshell.co.uk or something. I scrolled down the list. Bingo, there it was. Barbiebombshell@info.co.uk.

I opened a page for a new message and began to write:

```
Dear Kaylie,
I wanted to ask why you are being so horrible
to me. These last few weeks have been the worst
of my life and I've been really miserable . . .
```

I deleted that. It sounded too much like I was a victim.

```
Dear Kaylie,
Mahatma Gandhi said that in times of war, one
should try the peaceful methods of finding a
solution before resorting to fighting . . .
```

Definitely not. For one thing, Kaylie wouldn't know who Mahatma Gandhi was and would probably think that I was trying to be clever. Delete.

```
Dear Kaylie,
As you know these last few weeks have been
rather strained . . .
```

Rather *strained*? Understatement! When did I get to be so polite? I sounded like the blooming Queen! May husboind and A have been rather strained lately . . . it has been my annus horribilis. No. Definitely the wrong tone. Delete.

```
Dear Kaylie,
You finking stinking cow. You're making my life
hell — to the point that I don't want to come
to school any more. But I suppose that would
make you very happy, so you can stuff it. You're
not going to win, you rotten bitch. I don't know
why you've got it in for me, but LEAVE ME ALONE.
You stink, your hair's dyed and . . . and you've
got a big bum and short legs. And I bet that
they're hairy.
```

Hmmm. I *knew* I couldn't send that, but it did make me feel slightly better writing it. I quickly deleted it. With my luck, I'd press the wrong button and send it off by mistake!

After about twenty more versions, I finally wrote:

```
Dear Kaylie,
I don't understand why you have been so mean to
me the last few weeks or why you sent that
blatantly untrue note around our year. However,
I'm prepared to put it all behind me if you are.
Can we start again, make an effort to get on and
be friends?
Li@
```

There, I thought. Simple, to the point, and not too emotional. I pressed the send button before I could change my mind and off it went. I felt lighter than I had in days.

Half an hour later, Cat phoned.

'Are you on your own?' she asked.

'Yes. Why?'

There was a silence. Then Cat said, 'I don't know how to tell you this . . .'

I felt my chest tighten and the knot in my stomach twist. 'What?'

'I was just on the computer and I got mail. From Kaylie. I think she's sent the same message to everyone.'

'*What?* What did she say?'

'I wanted it to come from me and not anyone else.'

'I understand. What did she say?'

'She's written: *Ha ha, look at this. How pathetic. Poor little rich girl's got no friends.* Then she's pasted an e-mail from you asking if you could be friends with her. Did you write that?'

I felt sick. 'Yeah. Yeah, I did. I . . . I thought . . . oh, I don't know what I thought.'

'I'm so sorry, Lia. She's such a cow.'

'Yeah.'

'You *do* have friends. *I'm* your friend – you know that, don't you? And Becca. And Mac and Squidge. You don't need people like her. Or her approval.'

I knew she was right, but her words didn't console me. I didn't understand. Why were some people so horrible?

Two hours later, Becca phoned to tell me about the message. Apparently Mac and Squidge had got it as well.

'It looks like she's sent it to everyone from our school that has a computer,' said Becca.

'And that's just about everyone.'

'I'm going to kill her,' said Becca.

'Be my guest,' I said. 'I can't deal with it any more.'

Teen Queens and Has-beens 10

I CRIED myself to sleep that night and the next day woke with the now familiar knot in my stomach. I didn't want to go into school, but I daren't tell Mum. She'd soon realise why and storm in and have it out with the teachers. Another person waging war on my behalf was the last thing I needed. But then, my methods of trying to resolve things hadn't worked either. I felt ill. I didn't want to eat, didn't want to do anything but hide under the duvet and come out when it was all over and someone appeared at my bedside to tell me that it had all been a bad dream.

I made myself get up and get dressed, and then hoped that Mum and Dad would go out somewhere for the day and not notice that I hadn't gone in.

At half past eight, the doorbell rang. It was Squidge.

'Hey,' he said.

'Hey. What are you doing here?'

'Thought you might like someone to go into school with,' he said.

'But you've come right out of your way.'

'No problem,' he said.

'And Meena usually drives me.'

'Cool. I'll arrive in style.'

'Not if Max and Molly have their way,' I laughed. 'They'll be covered in mud.' The dogs had just spotted us from one of the lawns below the house and were running as fast as they could towards us. Squidge and I made a dive for the car, which was waiting outside one of the garages, ready to take me to school. We only just made it in time and couldn't help laughing at the disappointed looks on their faces as they put their paws up to the windows.

A few moments later, Meena appeared and we were on our way, leaving Max and Molly behind on the drive. As we got closer to school, I asked if he'd seen the message that Kaylie had sent round.

'Oh that.' He shrugged. 'That's what the delete button is for.'

Then he asked about what I was doing at the weekend and filled me in on the film he was making about the school show. We talked about music, what movies were coming out . . . everything apart from Kaylie and the Clones. By the time we got to school, the knot in my tummy had loosened a bit. Only when we got out of the car, did he refer to it.

'Don't let them wear you down, Lia,' he said. 'And you know where I am if you need me.'

As I walked towards class, Jackie came up behind me.

'Hey, Lia,' she said.

'Uh,' I replied, wondering what nastiness she had in store.

'How are you?'

What does she mean, how am I? I thought. She must know the effect that they've had on me these last two weeks.

'Look, Jackie, I don't know what you want, but if you want the truth, I've been very freaked out. I don't know why you and your mates are being so horrid to me. I've never done anything to you and I've had about as much as I can take.'

Jackie shook her head. 'I know. I feel rotten about it.'

I felt shocked. 'You do?'

'Yeah, course. Not everyone agrees with Kaylie all the time and I think she's been really mean to you. I'm sorry.'

This was the last thing I expected. 'Oh,' was all I could say.

'Yeah, a few of us feel bad about it. She can be a Class A bitch, can Kaylie.'

'Really,' I agreed. 'A total bitch.'

She gave me a friendly smile, then took off down the corridor. Strange, I thought. Not at all what I expected, but then maybe some of the Clones have got minds of their own after all. I made my way to the girls' cloakroom to sit for a minute on my own before facing everyone who had no doubt got Kaylie's e-mail the night before. I'd only been in there a few minutes when I heard the door open and voices. One of them was Kaylie's. I quickly lifted my feet off the floor so that she wouldn't know that I was in there.

'And did you see the way she wrote her name? Lia with an "at" symbol, like you use on e-mail addresses,' Kaylie was saying. 'I suppose she thinks she's pretty cool, doing that.'

'You thought it was cool before,' said Susie.

'I never did,' said Kaylie. 'Who's side are you on?'

'Yours, of course,' said Susie. 'I've always thought that she was full of herself, so stuck up. She makes me sick.'

'Yeah, with her designer clothes and her private chauffeur,' said Jackie.

That's Jackie's voice! I thought. But she was just so friendly to me and now she's slagging me off with the rest of them. What's going on?

But they weren't finished yet.

'And I bet her hair is dyed,' said Fran. 'No one has hair that blonde without spending some serious money on it.'

'Which we all know darling daddy has,' said Jackie. 'She probably thinks she can buy friends as well.'

'And she's such a show-off,' said Kaylie. 'With her *real*

Cartier watch. Like who cares? And why does she have to get driven to school every day in a Mercedes? Just to rub our noses in it. Like, look what I've got and you haven't. I mean, she could get the bus with the rest of us, but oh no, she wouldn't mix with us, would she?'

'I don't think she's that pretty anyway,' said Fran.

'No, me neither,' said Susie. 'Only in a really obvious way. Honestly, Kaylie, I couldn't believe that e-mail she sent you. What a cheek. Let's be friends – like, who'd want to be her friend?'

'And she didn't mean it,' said Jackie. 'I spoke to her two minutes ago in the hall and she said she thought you were a total bitch, Kaylie.'

'Really?' said Kaylie.

'Really. Her very words. "A total bitch." She was trying so hard to be friendly with me and get me on her side, but course, I wasn't having any of it.'

I felt my shoulders sag and I hung my head. So it was all an act from Jackie. Talk about two-faced! And to think for a moment, I'd thought she might be OK.

'No one will be her friend,' said Kaylie. 'Like it's *so* obvious that Cat and Becca only hang out with her because they wanted to get in with a famous family. If she wasn't Zac Axford's daughter, I bet they'd have nothing to do with her.

'Yeah,' said Fran, 'everyone knows that Cat only spends time with her because she wants to get off with her brother, Ollie.'

'And Mac and Squidge,' said Susie, 'they're such hangers-on. Wanting to be part of a glam lifestyle.'

'I bet she left her old school because she had no friends there either,' said Jackie.

'Yeah.'

'Yeah.'

'Poor little rich girl,' said Fran. 'I wonder if she knows she's a has-been.'

'We're the Teen Queens and she's the has-been,' said Kaylie, and they all started laughing.

Then I heard the door open and close again. I felt like I'd been stabbed in the stomach and the tears I'd been holding back started to fall. There was no way I could go into class after what I'd heard, especially with red, swollen eyes. I waited five minutes, until I heard the first bell go when I knew that they'd all be in assembly, then I ran for the door and out the school gates.

I went straight down to the Cremyl ferry, then caught the bus into Plymouth. I knew what I had to do next. They'd left me no option.

Becoming Invisible

11

'WHAT DO you mean, you don't want Meena to drive you to school any more?' asked Mum on Saturday morning as we had breakfast.

'There's a bus,' I said.

'But you'd have to walk about half a mile to get it. Don't be ridiculous, Lia. Meena's always taken you to school. What's this really about?'

I took a deep sigh and got ready to explain. My new tactic: I was going to do everything I could to fit in and *not* stand out, and that meant some things had to go. First, the chauffeur-driven lift to school. Second, my watch. I'd bought a new one at the market in Plymouth yesterday – cheap, pink strap, plastic. Third, my clothes. I'd got some new outfits from a discount warehouse – all for under a tenner. From now on, I'd wear my hair scraped back and no make-up. No one would be able to accuse me of showing off. I'd be grey, blend with the crowd. I was going to fit in if it killed me. In fact, more than that; I was going to be invisible so that no one would notice me at all.

'It's really important that I don't stand out in any way, Mum. Being the only one at school who is chauffeur-driven in a Mercedes makes me stand *way* out.'

'But loads of the kids get dropped off or picked up.'

'Yeah, but not in this year's Mercedes. And the others get picked up by their mums and dads – not by the housekeeper.'

'Are you saying you want me to drive you in?'

'Yes. *No.*' Mum drives a silver Porsche. Imagine what they'd make of that! 'No. But how about Meena drives me in in her car? Her old Ford wouldn't stand out so much.'

'Has that girl been getting at you again?'

'No,' I lied. 'I just want to fit in, and it's so different to my old school, that's all.'

Mum didn't look like she believed me. 'Well, you're going to have to wear a paper bag over your head, Lia. You're a stunning girl, and I'm not just saying that because I'm your mum. You'll always stand out in a crowd.'

'Not if I dress down and don't wear any make-up.'

'Lia, have you looked in the mirror lately? You look just as good without make-up as you do with it on.'

'I have to blend in, Mum. It's really important. Please support me on this.'

Mum sighed. 'I'm not happy about this, Lia. Something's

not right and I get the feeling that you're not telling me the whole story, but . . . if that's what you want, then fine. I do understand how important it is at your age not to feel like the odd one out. So Meena will take you in her car from now on. And you're going to wear drab clothes . . . I don't get it, but fine.'

It seemed to work to a degree. Nothing major happened. The Clones just ignored me or sniggered if I ever said anything within their earshot. I could deal with that. I no longer wore anything to school that would draw attention to me. I stopped putting my hand up in class when a teacher asked a question. Meena picked me up in her old banger. I made sure I saw Jonno out of school and kept out of his way in school. If I saw Kaylie or one of the Clones coming, I'd turn and walk the other way. They'd won, they knew it, and they seemed to lose interest.

As the weeks went on and life settled down, I carried on seeing Jonno. However as I began to feel slightly better, I also began to feel that Jonno and I didn't have much in common. I found I was making excuses so that I could hang out with the old crowd – Mac, Becca, Squidge and Cat. Jonno preferred coming up to the house to going out, so he could watch the footie with Dad, and it just wasn't fun like it was with my mates.

We did spend a little time on our own, though – going for a pizza, to a movie, round the Old Town in Plymouth. Those were the times when I began to realise that it wasn't really happening for me with him. We didn't talk in the way that I've been able to talk with boyfriends in the past and, some of the time, I felt like Jonno was just agreeing with me and not really listening when I tried to share some of my ideas or views about things. There were only two topics of conversation that Jonno was interested in: sport and music. And it was getting boring. That and his new joke collection, which had made me laugh in the beginning, but was starting to wear a bit thin. Every time I saw him, he had a new one for me.

'How do you make Kaylie's eyes light up? Shine a torch in her ear.'

'Why does Kaylie hate Smarties? Because they're hard to peel.'

'What's the difference between a Kaylie Clone and a supermarket trolley? A supermarket trolley has a mind of its own.'

'What does a Kaylie Clone do when someone shouts, "There's a mouse in the room!"? Checks her highlights.'

'What's the similarity between a Brazilian rainforest and Kaylie O'Hara? They're both dense.'

And on and on they went. I think he got the jokes from the Internet, then adapted them. I think the jokes were his way of being supportive, but as the weeks went on, I was beginning to wish he'd just shut up about Kaylie. I didn't even want to hear her name.

Thank God for Squidge. He phoned one Saturday afternoon when Dad and Jonno were ensconced in their usual positions on the sofa and asked if I'd go up to Rame Head with him.

I leaped at the chance. We took the dogs with us and had one of the best afternoons I've had in ages. Cat told me that Squidge plans to do a film about the tiny church up there. It's right on the peninsula, on top of a small hill that looks out over the sea. There's something about the place. It's magical. I always feel so peaceful there, like nothing in the world matters.

'So how's it going with lover boy?' he asked as we made our way up the steps to the church.

'Och, he's football crazy,' I sang in a Scottish accent. 'Football mad.'

Squidge laughed. 'Not your scene, huh?'

'No thanks. I think he should be dating my dad – they're clearly madly in love.'

'It must be hard for you sometimes . . .'

'What do you mean?'

'All the trappings that come with you. Fab house. Your dad. You must get hangers-on.'

'Yeah. In fact, I overheard Kaylie and the Clones saying

that you and Mac were only interested in me because of the glam lifestyle.'

I expected him to laugh it off, but Squidge looked serious. 'Just be careful, Lia,' he said. 'Sometimes you don't know who your real friends are.'

I wasn't sure who he was talking about, but I didn't want to pursue it and ruin our afternoon. It did make me wonder, though. Cat? Becca? Mac? Who was he referring to?

Gutted

12

THE FOLLOWING Tuesday morning, I was going into school as normal and spotted Cat and Becca just inside the gates. They were deeply engrossed in conversation about something and didn't see me until I'd almost got up to them.

Becca jumped as soon as she saw me and nudged Cat to shut her up.

'Oh,' said Cat, looking awkward. 'Lia.'

'What were you talking about?' I asked. 'You looked totally absorbed.'

Becca glanced guiltily at Cat. 'Oh, nothing,' she said.

'Um, we were talking about the show,' said Cat.

Yeah right, I thought. My heart sank. I knew they were lying.

As we walked into school together, I felt gutted, even more so when I saw Cat look at Becca and make a face, as if to say, Oh dear, she almost caught us. I felt like turning around and running. It was the last betrayal. Cat and Becca, my two best friends. And now even they were talking about me in secret.

It was too much. I no longer knew who to trust. I was beginning to think that maybe changing schools had been the worst idea of my whole life. I resolved that when I got home, I'd speak to Mum about going back to my old school. I had my friends up there and even though it would mean being away from home again and I'd miss Mum and Dad, at least Star and Ollie were in London and I'd be away from this nightmare.

In the break, I went off to find Squidge. At first, I thought that I wouldn't say anything to him as I know that Cat and Becca are his friends too, but somehow I felt I could trust him. He had tried to warn me about who my real friends were.

'I just don't understand it,' I said after I explained what I'd seen. 'I really thought that there were no secrets between Cat, Bec and me, and now . . . I don't know what to think. They were clearly talking about me.'

Squidge shook his head. 'No. You've got it wrong. They *are* your mates. Honest. Look, they were probably trying to protect you.'

'Against what?'

'Same ole, same ole. Kaylie.'

'No,' I said. 'She's been OK lately. Lost interest.'

'I don't think so . . .'

'Why?'

Squidge bit his lip.

'Oh, please Squidge. If they're doing something I don't know about, please tell me. Please.'

'Look, promise you won't say that I told you . . .'

'Promise.'

'Apparently Kaylie's still trying to stir it about you. She told Cat and Becca that you'd been slagging them off to her.'

'*What?* I never even speak to Kaylie. That's mad!'

Squidge shrugged. 'Well, she is, isn't she?'

'How do you know this? When did it happen?'

'Last night at rehearsal. I saw her talking to Cat and Becca, then Becca told me what she'd said.'

My stomach tightened into the familiar knot. 'And what did she say?'

'Something about you saying that you only hung out with Cat and Becca because they were nice to you when you first arrived and now you can't shake them off. Then she told them that really you wanted to be in with Kaylie and her lot and that's why you've been so upset about them not accepting you.'

'But surely they wouldn't believe her? I'd never slag them off. Why didn't they phone and ask me? Why didn't they tell me about it this morning?'

Squidge faced me squarely and put his hands on my

shoulders. 'Because they didn't believe a word of it and didn't want to upset you. Look, Lia. They're your best mates. They know what Kaylie's like.'

'Do they? *Do* they? But they were whispering about me this morning. I just don't know who to trust any more. And . . . and on Saturday, you said to be careful about who my real friends were.'

'I didn't mean *them*, you doofus,' said Squidge.

'Then who?'

This time it was Squidge's turn to look uncomfortable.

'Who?' I insisted.

Squidge hesitated for what seemed like ages. 'OK. Jonno,' he said finally.

'Why? He's not in with Kaylie,' I said. 'He doesn't even like her.'

'I know,' said Squidge. 'Look, forget I even said anything. It's probably just me coming over all big brothery about you.'

'Oh, tell me, Squidge. Do you know something about Jonno that I don't?'

Squidge glanced around the playground to make sure no one was listening. 'Not exactly. Just . . . you know what we were talking about on Saturday. About hangers-on. Well, sorry, but I think that's what Jonno might be doing. When you talk about him, it sounds like he used you to get in with your dad. You know he's desperate to get into the music business when he leaves here. He must know that your dad could help him and it sounds like he spends more time with him than you.'

I couldn't deny it. It had begun to really annoy me lately, and privately, I had been thinking of calling it a day with him. Not so much because I thought he was a hanger-on, but because I didn't think I really fancied him any more. There was no chemistry – not on my side anyway. Even though he was good looking and nice, I wanted more than that. I preferred to be with someone I could really talk to and have a laugh with, and if I had a boyfriend, I wanted one who made me feel tingly when he kissed me. Snogging Jonno was like eating porridge. A bit dull.

'I hope I haven't spoken out of turn,' said Squidge anxiously. 'In fact, take no notice of me. Deep down, I'm probably jealous.'

'Jealous?'

Now Squidge looked *really* awkward. 'Look, got to go. Class starts in a minute.' And with that, he turned and fled.

Squidge jealous? That stopped me in my tracks for a minute. Could he possibly fancy me? I felt my brain do a gear shift, as I'd never let myself imagine being with him. But we do get on well. He's so funny and full of life and new ideas, and he has the most amazing brown eyes, with thick black lashes and a lovely wide mouth . . . Hmm. Jealous? Maybe he felt the same about me. Yes, interesting. Very interesting.

13 Vicars and Tarts

'SO PLEASE, no secrets,' I said to Cat and Becca when I caught up with them at lunch-time. 'I know that Kaylie was stirring it again, but please, tell me when she tries a stunt like that.'

'We didn't want you getting upset,' said Becca. 'And it wasn't as if we took any notice. In fact, Cat asked how many times she'd have to flush before Kaylie would go away.'

I laughed. 'I'd be more upset if I thought you weren't my mates any more. I knew something was going on when I saw you this morning. I felt awful. I thought I'd lost you. I'm sorry, I guess I'm getting paranoid with everything that's been going on, so please, no secrets from each other.'

Cat looked at Becca questioningly and Becca gave her a nod.

'We were talking about you, Lia,' she said. 'It's true. But not what you think. We weren't talking about Kaylie – I wouldn't waste my breath. No. We were trying to think of a surprise for you. We know you've had a rough time lately, and we wanted to do something to cheer you up.'

'Just be my friends and always tell me what's going on. That's the best thing you could ever do.'

'Yeah, but we wanted to do *something* . . . I don't know,' sighed Becca. 'It's like you haven't been yourself lately. You've been sort of defeated, like a shadow of yourself. You're so quiet. You can even see it in your posture. You've stooped in on yourself – it's as though you're trying to disappear.'

'I am,' I said. 'I don't want anyone to notice me.'

'But that's not you,' said Cat. 'It's like Kaylie's rubbing you out somehow. We wanted to do something to bring the old Lia back. Make you laugh again.'

'Like what?'

Well, that's what we were trying to decide. A movie, a sleepover . . . dunno. We didn't know if you'd like to do something on your own or whether you'd want Jonno along.'

'OK, seeing as we're being totally honest, I don't think I want to go out with Jonno any more.'

'Why?' asked Becca.

I shrugged. 'Don't know. I mean, he's a really nice guy and cute and everything, but I don't think we've got a lot in common.'

'This isn't part of your campaign to be invisible, is it?' asked Becca. 'You've ditched the watch, the nice clothes, the Mercedes and now you're going to ditch the cutest boy in school, all so that Kaylie O'Horrible won't give you a hard time . . .'

Speak of the devil. At that very moment, Kaylie came out of the loos and made a beeline for us. In her hand, she had a pile of envelopes. Oh, here we go, I thought. Invites to one of her do's.

'Hi.' She smiled at us all, then turned to me and handed me an invite. 'Look, Lia, I just wanted to say, let's bury the hatchet and start again. I've been thinking about that e-mail you sent and you're right, we should try to get on. So, bygones be bygones, etc., and please come to my party on Saturday.'

I think my mouth fell open. 'Oh . . . right. Thanks,' I said as I took the envelope from her.

She gave invites to Cat and Becca as well. 'I thought I'd have a theme party this time,' she said, 'so it's fancy dress. Vicars and Tarts. All the boys are coming as vicars, so all the girls are coming as tarts. Should be a right laugh.'

Becca pulled a face at her as she went off. 'What a cheek! I don't believe it. At rehearsal, she fed us a pack of lies about you and now she swans in and gives us invites as though nothing was said. Huh! Bury the hatchet? Her? More like she wants to bury it in our backs. So no. No way

I'm going to one of her stupid parties. Not if you paid me.'

'Me neither,' said Cat. 'She might think she can just wave and we'll all come running. No way. No, let's put these invites in the bin.'

'No, wait,' I said. 'I think we should go. She's put out the hand of friendship and I bet that wasn't easy for someone like her. Please. I don't want to go on my own, so please come with me. I . . . I want to give it a try.'

Becca looked at Cat.

'Why is getting on with Kaylie so important to you, Lia?' asked Becca. 'She's a Class A bitch. You don't need people like that in your life.'

I felt a moment's panic. I didn't want them to think that there was any truth in what Kaylie had said to them about me wanting to get in with her and shake them off.

'I don't want to be a close friend of hers, I don't. I just want it to be all right between us. Like, no stuff . . . no bad vibes. If she is on the level and I don't go to her do, she might think I'm being snooty or something. I'd like to go and show that I simply want to get on with everyone. Then maybe we can put this whole mad thing behind us all and get on with our lives.'

'All right,' sighed Becca. 'But only for you.'

On the night of the party, we had a great laugh getting dressed. Being Queen Party Planner, Mum's got a dressing-up chest full of weird and wonderful costumes from Venetian wigs to Japanese kimonos to Roman togas. At the bottom of the chest, we found some wonderful tarty gear. Rubber skirts, feather boas, blonde wigs, high strappy shoes . . . Becca put on a tiny black leather skirt and black lace bra with a see-through black blouse over it. Cat chose a white see-through top with a black bra underneath – very trashy. And I went for a short, low cut, pink strappy dress, fishnet tights and a magenta pink feather boa. We plastered our faces with make-up and back-combed our hair as high as we could. By the time we'd finished we looked like a right bunch of slappers.

Dad's eyes almost came out on stalks when he saw us totter down the stairs in our high heels. 'And just where on earth do you think you're going, dressed like that?' he asked.

'Party,' said Cat.

'I don't think so . . .' Dad began.

'Fancy dress,' I said. 'Vicars and Tarts, and I think you can tell that we're not the vicars.'

He still didn't seem too happy about it. 'Put your coats on until you get there and I'll drive you.' He glanced anxiously at the three of us again. '*And* pick you up!'

I asked Dad to drop us on the corner of Kaylie's road, as I didn't want to draw attention to his Ferrari. As soon as he drove off, we whipped off our coats, applied a bit more rouge and red lipstick, then tottered up to Kaylie's front door. Becca rang the bell.

A few moments later, a middle-aged lady with frizzy blond hair answered the door. She was wearing a tracksuit and smoking a cigarette. She looked horrified to see us standing there, giggling, on her doorstep.

She took a drag of her cigarette. 'Yeah?'

Suddenly I had a sense of foreboding. There was no sound of music coming from inside or people's voices. The house was quiet and I could see a flicker of light from a TV through the window at the front.

Becca and Cat began suspect something was up at the same time. 'I . . . er, we thought there was a party here,' said Becca.

'Well, you thought wrong,' said Mrs O'Hara, looking us up and down with disapproval. 'And do your parents know that you're out dressed like this?'

'Um, we thought it was fancy dress,' muttered Cat. 'Sorry. Wrong house. Sorry to have bothered you.'

Mrs O'Hara shut the door without another word. She doesn't look like a very friendly person, I thought, walking down the path towards the gate. Suddenly, I was blinded by a flash of light as someone leaped out of nowhere.

'Smile for the camera,' called Kaylie. As my eyes adjusted back to the dark, I could see that behind her were the

Clones – Jackie, Fran and Susie. They were all laughing their heads off. Becca put her hand up to her face so that they couldn't get another picture, but it was too late, Kaylie was clicking away as fast as she could.

Suddenly Becca made a bolt for her, but she wasn't quick enough to get the camera. Kaylie ran for her front door and in a second, disappeared inside. The Clones raced down the road to the left and were out of sight in a minute.

'Come on,' cried Becca, setting off after them, 'let's get them.'

Cat and I tried to follow them, but in three-inch high heels, running was an impossibility. Cat collapsed into a privet hedge in someone's front garden and starting laughing.

'I can't even walk in these things, never mind run,' she moaned.

Becca came back to check that Cat was OK, then looked in the direction that the Clones had gone. 'Oh, stuff them,' said Becca. 'They're not worth it.'

'Yeah,' I said. 'Stuff them.' She put her arm around me. 'It doesn't matter, Lia. Who needs Kaylie or her stupid friends anyway?'

'Yeah,' said Cat. 'So she got us to dress up – like, very funny, ha ha.'

'Yeah, pathetic,' I agreed.

'Let's go back to yours, Lia, and have our own party,' said Cat.

We all sat on the wall and, as I got out my mobile to call Dad, a green Fiesta drove past. It slowed down when the driver saw us.

'Whey *hey*,' called a boy in the passenger seat as he wound down his window. 'Want to spend the rest of your lives with me, darlin's?'

'You couldn't afford my dry cleaning, *darling*,' Cat called back in a very posh voice.

When they realised that we weren't interested, they drove off, thankfully. Cat and Becca began to laugh and I tried to join in, but my earlier sense of foreboding had deepened. Somehow I felt that this wasn't the end of it.

14 The Last Straw

THE FOLLOWING Monday, when I got into school, there was a crowd of people around the notice board in the corridor outside the assembly hall. There seemed to be a lot of giggling going on, so I went to see what the joke was. People often posted jokes that they'd found on the internet, although they didn't last long up there, as usually one of the teachers saw them and took them down. As I approached, one of the boys in the crowd spotted me and nudged the person next to him. Suddenly, everyone went quiet. Kaylie, I thought immediately. Oh no, what has she done now? The crowd parted like a wave and I peered at the board to see what they'd all been looking at. Up on the board was a blown-up Polaroid of Cat, Becca and me, dressed in our tarts' outfits. Underneath it, was written: *The real Lia Axford and her mates. How the little Miss Perfects are out of school. We vote for Ophelia Axford as Slag of the Week. Sign here if you agree.'* There was a whole list of names and a few messages with boys' phone numbers with invitations to call them.

Jerry Robinson from Year Eight whistled and winked. 'Hey, Ophelia, I'll have afeelofya. Get it?' he started laughing. 'Ophelia, a feel of ya. And you look so quiet in school. Call me.' Then he laughed. 'No, on second thoughts, I'll call you. Maybe.'

I tried to smile and make light of it, but inside I felt frozen. I couldn't even cry. This was the last straw. I felt numb except for the knot in my stomach that felt tighter than ever. Suddenly, I couldn't breathe. As the crowd dispersed, I reached up to take down the photo. Just as I reached out, someone put a hand on my shoulder. It was Miss Segal.

'I'll take that,' she said with a grim expression. She took the photo from the board and walked off without a second glance at me.

That's it, I thought as I watched her walk away. My favourite teacher and now even *she* is going to think badly of me. I ran for the girls' cloakrooms and luckily they were empty. The bell went for assembly and I could hear everyone outside heading for the hall. I went into the last cubicle and locked the door. I'd reached the end. I didn't know how to be any more.

First, the boys here thought I was aloof, and now they

thought that I was a slag. I'd tried standing up for myself. I'd tried being invisible. None of it had worked and now Kaylie had even got it in for Cat and Becca and it was all because of me. If I hadn't come to this school, I thought, their photo wouldn't be up on the notice board for the whole world to see. I felt a total failure. I'd let everyone down. I didn't fit in here. And it was probably my fault. So that was it. I would definitely, *definitely* talk to Mum about leaving this horrible school and going back to my old one in London.

I decided to hide in the cubicle until assembly got going, then I would go home and beg Mum to let me leave here and never come back.

It was only a minute later that I heard the cloakroom door open then close. Like before, when Kaylie and her mates came in, I lifted my feet up so that no one would know I was in there. This is insane, I thought, I can't stay at this school any longer. I can't spend the rest of my school years hiding in the loos.

Whoever it was that had come in was looking in each cubicle. Oh, *please* don't be Kaylie, I prayed. I didn't think I could take any more of her abuse.

'Lia, I know you're in here.'

It was Squidge's voice! What should I do, I asked myself . . . ? Maybe if I'm really quiet, he'll go away. He reached the cubicle I was in and tried the door.

'Lia?'

I tried not to breathe.

'Lia. I know you're in there. Look. No one takes Kaylie and her mob seriously. You mustn't take it to heart. Honestly, no one gives a toss. Please come out.'

A moment later, the cloakroom doors opened again and I heard more footsteps.

'Is she in here?' asked Mac.

'Lia?' called Becca.

'I think she's in there,' said Squidge.

It wasn't that I didn't want to speak to them – I just couldn't. I felt numb.

'Hey, Lia,' said Cat softly. 'We know you've seen the photo. So they think they've made fools of us. It's no biggie. We're in this together. Please come out.'

'Yeah, in fact,' said Becca, 'most people think she's a sad loser, stooping to this last stunt. Come on, come out.'

I didn't reply.

'We're not going to go away,' said Squidge.

I heard footsteps go into the cubicle next door and it sounded like someone was hoisting themselves up. Suddenly there was Becca's face peering over the partition. She smiled. 'Hey, we've got to stop meeting like this.'

'Is she in there?' asked Cat.

'Yeah,' said Becca. 'Come on, Lia, come out. We can deal with this. Together. Come on.'

I felt so ashamed. So stupid and weak that I couldn't be like them and just laugh it off.

'Come on,' said Becca. 'You can't sit in here all day. Assembly will be over in a minute and people will start coming in before class.'

'I'm so sorry,' I whispered. I got up and unlocked the door. I still didn't feel like going out, but on hearing the lock open, Cat pushed the door and came in and put her arm around me.

'You're bigger than this,' she said. 'Come on. We have to show them that it hasn't got to us. We can't let her win.'

'I'm so sorry,' I said again. 'I wish I could be like you, but . . . I'm sorry. It's like I've just, I dunno . . . I'm going to go back to my old school. I can't take it here any more . . .'

Suddenly Mac stiffened and jerked his thumb towards the door. We all held our breath for a moment as we listened to the footsteps outside in the corridor. Click clack on the floor. Quick footsteps. Alert. Efficient. Not the footsteps of a schoolgirl or boy sauntering to or from assembly. The door opened. It was the headmistress.

'Becca Howard. Why aren't you in assembly? Jack Squires and Tom Macey! *What* are you doing in the girls' cloakrooms? And who's in that cubicle?' She marched forward. 'Cat Kennedy. Lia Axford.' She sniffed the air. 'You've not been smoking, have you?'

'No, Miss,' said Becca.

Mrs Harvey looked us all up and down. 'I don't expect this sort of behaviour from any of you lot. Don't let me see it again!'

Then she turned on her spiky heels and left.

I was still ready to make a bolt for home, but Squidge wouldn't let me leave.

'You know that saying. Take a twig on its own and it's easy to snap. Bind a few twigs together, not so easy to break. Five twigs, even more difficult. There's you, me, Mac, Cat and Becca. They won't break us if we stick together. You're not alone in this. OK?'

'OK . . .' I said, with an attempt at a smile. Dear Squidge, I thought. He's trying his best, and maybe even thought he fancied me, but he doesn't know what I'm like. Pathetic. A loser. Can't fight my own battles. Whingey, wet and full of self-pity. It's best I'm out of here and out of all their lives.

Cat and Becca wouldn't let me go. They marched me, one on either side, to the first class. Although Kaylie and the Clones sniggered when we walked in, it didn't matter any more. I'd decided. Her, her clones and this horrible episode were soon going to be nothing more than a bad memory. Three classes to sit through: double English, then drama with Miss Segal. Then at lunch, I'd slip away. I'd go back to my old school and, at last, the nightmare would be over for good.

15 Role-play Nightmare

'OK, CLASS,' said Miss Segal, looking around the room. I tried not to meet her eyes as I felt embarrassed about the photo she'd taken from the board. 'Today I want to do something a bit different. I know we've done scripts in the past, we've looked at other people's words, other people's ideas. Today, we going to free things up a bit.'

I was hardly listening. In my head, I was calling my old mates in London – Tara, Athina, Gabby, Sienna, Olivia, Isobel and Natalie. I hoped they would still be my friends when I went back to my old school, and that they'd still like me and accept me and not pick up on the fact that, somehow, I'd become a loser.

'Lia?' asked Miss Segal. 'Are you with us today?'

I nodded. 'Sorry. Yes. Just thinking.'

Kaylie sniggered. It didn't bother me. You're history, I thought. I only have to get through this last class, then

I'll never ever have to see you or your stupid friends ever again.

'Right,' continued Miss Segal. 'We're going to do some role-play situations. I'll need a couple of volunteers, then I'll set the scene and we'll see where it takes us. The idea is to improvise. I'm not going to tell you what to say or do, just see what comes into your head.'

Count me out, I thought. One thing I will not be doing today is volunteering for anything like that. Sounds like my worst nightmare.

'OK. First scenario,' said Miss Segal. 'Two people who have some kind of a relationship. What it is, our volunteers have to decide. It can be sisters, family, business partners, whatever. It can be at home, in an office, school . . . you choose, and the rest of us will try and work out what the relationship is. OK. Who's up?'

Mary Andrews and Mark Keegan put their hands up. I watched as though from a distance as they enacted a scene in a bank. It was quite clear. Mark was the manager and Mary was a customer. I wasn't really interested. I looked at my watch. Thirty-five minutes to go until lunch-time. Then I was out of here.

After Mark and Mary had done their role-play, Miss Segal stood up again. 'Good,' she said. 'Now let's make it more interesting. The essence of all good drama is conflict. And how do you create that?'

'Fight, Miss,' said Joanne Nesbitt.

'Arguments,' said Bill Malloy.

'Yes, but what causes those arguments in the first place?' asked Miss Segal.

No one answered.

'Conflict of some sort,' said Miss Segal. 'By putting opposites together we can create that. For example, put two non-smokers on a train. What do we have?'

'People with something in common,' said David Alexander.

'OK. Two smokers together?' asked Miss Segal.

'A smoky compartment,' said Mark Keegan.

Miss Segal laughed. 'Yes, but again, we have two people who get on. Now. Put a smoker and a non-smoker in a room together and what do we have?'

Becca gave Kaylie a dirty look. 'Conflict,' she said.

'That's right. Can anyone think of any other opposites?'

'Vegetarian and meat-eater,' said Sunita Ahmed.

'Good. Any others?'

'Different religions, different politics . . .' said Laura Johnson.

'That's it. Now you're getting it.'

'Rich and poor,' said Cat.

'Popular and not popular,' sneered Kaylie, with a side glance at me.

'Winner and loser,' said Susie.

'Excellent. So, for our next scenario,' continued Miss Segal, 'I want two boys.'

Peter Hounslow and Scott Parker got up and went to the front.

'OK, boys, this time I want you to play opposites. You choose who and where. Let it evolve and let's see what happens.'

Despite myself, I couldn't help but be interested. In front of me, Pete and Scott began to size each other up, then call each other names. Pete started mocking Scott's voice and laughing at him. It wasn't long before the boys were fighting. I knew it wasn't serious as they're best friends out of school, but it reminded me that when a boy is a bully, then it's obvious. Pete was playing the bully and Scott was his victim.

When they'd finished, Miss Segal clapped. 'Excellent, and did you see, as they got into their roles, Pete became stronger and Scott became weaker? Great body language, boys. Scott, you really looked weary and defeated by the end. OK. I think that was pretty clear – the bully and his victim.'

She looked around class and fixed her gaze on me. 'OK. Now let's see how two girls might play out that situation.'

I felt myself stiffen. This was getting a bit close to home and I felt like I wanted to disappear. No way. Look somewhere else, I thought as I stared at the floor, avoiding

Miss Segal's eyes. I felt myself getting hot. I looked at my watch. Only twenty more minutes to go.

Miss Segal's gaze moved on. 'Any volunteers?'

To my amazement, Cat nodded at Becca, then the two of them were up like a shot.

'OK, girls,' said Miss Segal. 'Off you go.'

Cat started to say something and Becca started rolling her eyes and looking away as if she was really bored. She flicked her hair and sniggered to an invisible person. Cat shut up. Then Becca started acting really friendly to a group of invisible people and pretended to hand out cards. She stopped at Cat. 'Oh sorry, not you,' she said, with a toss of her hair. 'You're not pretty enough.'

Someone at the back laughed. I was stunned. She was doing the most perfect imitation of Kaylie. Then Becca walked into Cat. 'Oh *sorry*, wasn't looking where I was going,' she said, with a really false smile. Cat started looking miserable. 'Oh, lighten up, Cat,' teased Becca. 'You're too serious.'

I glanced over at Kaylie. She was looking daggers at Becca. I wanted to die. Becca was on a roll. She spoke to her invisible friends, sniggered, whispered, gave Cat filthy looks.

Finally, she stood in front of Cat with her hand on her hip. 'Whatever kind of style you were going for,' she said, 'you missed.' Then she started laughing again.

When they'd finished, Miss Segal clapped. 'Well done,'

120

she said. 'And very interesting. I'll tell you why. Because with the first scenario, the boys, it was clear. Pete was the bully, Scott was the victim. But with Cat and Becca, it felt different. Can anyone tell me why?'

A hush had fallen over the class. A few girls glanced nervously at Kaylie.

Miss Segal looked around. I think she felt the tension in the air. 'It's suddenly gone very quiet in here. Come on, class. Why did it feel different?'

Sunita put up her hand. 'With the boys, the bullying was physical. With the girls, it was more subtle. Like, Scott would have had a bruise or a broken arm to show for it. All Cat had was a broken ego. The aggression towards her was almost unseen, as Becca made it all look so casual. Like walking into her accidentally on purpose. Cat might think that she was imagining it.'

'So, what's the solution?' asked Miss Segal.

'There isn't one,' said Sunita. 'You can't tell your parents, as it's not like you've got a black eye or anything, and if you make a fuss, they might make things worse by causing a scene at school and *no one* wants that.'

'So why not go to a teacher?' asked Miss Segal.

'No way,' said Laura Johnson. 'What are you going to say? They might think, What's the big deal? So someone walked into you or didn't invite you to their party. So what. Deal with it. Then you'd feel like a fool. Or maybe the teacher would talk to the bully girl and then the girl might act all sugary-nice to you for a while, but you'd know it was totally false. No, best leave teachers out of it.'

I had the feeling that Sunita and Laura were talking from experience and wondered whether they had once been subject to Kaylie's methods as well.

'So what *do* you do?' asked Miss Segal.

No one spoke for a few moments, then a voice from the back of the classroom started up. It was Tina Woods, a really quiet girl who hardly ever said anything. 'You, er . . .' She nervously adjusted her glasses. 'You cry at home on your own. You hide your feelings and try and get through each day without anyone noticing you . . . You try to be invisible.'

At that moment, the bell went for lunch and people began to shuffle at their desks, anxious to get out, but I was riveted to my seat. Tina had described my experience exactly, as had Laura and Sunita.

'Just before you go,' said Miss Segal, 'I'd like to say that there *are* things that you can do. Most bullies are cowards at heart and must be stood up to, one way or another. Expose them. Because if they're doing it to one person, they're probably doing it to someone else as well. And if not now, they will in another year. I should know. I was bullied at school and it took me a long time to realise that I had to be myself and not to let others define who I was.

OK, you can go now, but I'm here if anyone wants to talk about this further.'

As the class made a dash for the door, I noticed that Tina Woods was hovering in the background. I got up and followed Cat and Becca out the door. I felt stunned.

16 Real Friends

'YOU WERE totally brilliant, Becca,' said Laura as we sat eating our sandwiches in the hall at lunch-time. 'You had you-know-who down to a T.'

Everyone was talking about Miss Segal's class. It seemed that loads of people had stories about being bullied. Tina, Sunita, Laura – even some of the boys had been subject to forms of exclusion, name calling and general nastiness.

'Well, I'm not afraid to say her name,' said Cat. 'You mean Kaylie. And it's the first time I've ever seen her look so uncomfortable in class. And I noticed she scarpered pretty fast when the bell went. Doesn't want a taste of her own medicine.'

'She and her mates made my life miserable last term, just because I wore the wrong kind of trainers,' said Sunita. 'But my parents couldn't afford to buy me the trendy ones.'

'So what did you do?' asked Cat.

'I begged my mum and she saved up and got me some new ones for Christmas,' said Sunita, 'but that didn't work either. Kaylie accused me of being a copycat and dressing like her.'

'You can't win with people like her,' said Becca. 'Best just leave them to rot in their own poison.'

'It's amazing,' I said, 'because there were times when I thought it was just me. That it was my fault.'

'No way,' said Becca. 'There are just some girls who are really mean. Who knows the reason. Like Jade Macey. We could have been real mates. But no, she didn't want anyone else from our school going for that Pop Princess competition. And she was just plain horrible to anyone she saw as a threat.'

'I hate all that,' I said. 'Why can't people just see each other as equals, not as rivals.'

'Way too liberal for someone like Kaylie,' said Cat. 'She sees you as a threat, especially as you took Jonno from under her nose . . .'

'Well, she can have him back.' I laughed. 'Actually, no. Even though I don't want to go out with him, he's still too nice for Kaylie.'

'Still want to leave, Lia?' asked Cat.

I looked at my watch and shook my head. It was ten to one. My plan to run as soon as morning classes ended had been forgotten. Miss Segal's class had changed everything. I realised that I wasn't alone.

'So, what are we going to do to stop her antics from now on?' asked Becca. 'She's made the best part of this term a misery for Lia, and for Tina, Laura, Sunita and probably a load of others too.'

'Confront her, Lia,' said Cat. 'I bet there's enough people to back you up. She'd run a mile. She's OK if she can get you on your own or if she's got her little gang with her, but I bet she wouldn't be so sure of herself if she realised that she's outnumbered.'

I shook my head. 'After this morning, I honestly don't think it's going to be necessary. There's no doubt that everyone in our class knew what was going on. Her behaviour has been exposed all right, and I doubt if she'll be able to get away with it in future.'

'I guess,' said Cat. 'In fact, I think everyone can see what a spiteful cow she is and always has been. I think you'll be surprised at how much anti-Kaylie feeling there is.'

'Count me in,' said Laura.

'And me,' said Sunita, taking a seat next to me and offering me a piece of her Kit Kat.

I felt hugely relieved, as until today I'd thought that Sunita and Laura didn't like me either. I thought no one did. And now I saw that it wasn't that they didn't like me. Kaylie had a hold over a good number of people and they were afraid to go against her. What a waste. All that time worrying what these girls thought about me and we might have been friends all along.

I took a deep breath. 'And do you know, the fact that I let it all get to me so much suddenly seems mad. I don't even like Kaylie . . .'

'Neither do we,' said Laura and Sunita in unison.

'So why have I been so bothered about whether I fit in with her crowd or not?' I said. 'I don't want her as a friend. It's weird – it seemed so important to win her over, but I see now I'll never win her over. And you know what? I *don't* care.'

'That's exactly what I realised with Jade,' said Becca. 'I have some really good mates – you and Cat and the boys – and there I was, getting all strung out about some stupid girl who was just mean. Not someone I wanted to hang out with anyway. It *is* weird, you're right. It can get all out of proportion. We spend so much time wanting to be liked by people who we don't even like ourselves.'

Laura started laughing.

'It's true,' said Laura. 'It's because they're popular . . .'

'Not so popular after today, I don't think,' said Cat. 'And who said they were popular anyway? I think it's a myth they started themselves.'

'It worked,' said Laura. 'Because they didn't like me, I thought no one did. Just because I don't dress and behave like them, they made me feel like I was a weirdo. I wish they could accept that everyone is different and just let people be.'

'Yeah, there's room for all of us,' said Sunita, then she laughed. 'Not everyone wants to be a Barbie and it's not a look I could ever really do – not unless I bleached my skin and dyed my hair.'

'Yeah,' said Laura. 'We don't all have to be like her to have friends. There are plenty of people in our year, and only four of them.'

'Exactly,' said Becca. 'I think it's important to invest in the people you do like – your real friends. It's what they think that counts.'

I nodded. 'That's what my dad said, but I didn't really appreciate it at the time. He was right. There will always be people for and against you and it's pointless wasting time trying to win over some of the people who are against. Spend time with the people who are *for* you. Those relationships are worth it.'

'And that means being totally honest so that we always know that we can trust each other,' said Cat. 'Even if what we say upsets the other. I think trust is the most important thing there is.'

'No hiding anything,' said Becca.

'And no unspoken grievances, as that's how it all starts,' I added. 'So no secrets.'

I felt happier than I had in weeks, like a huge weight had been lifted. At that moment, Squidge appeared at the end of the table and I suddenly found myself blushing. Ohmigod, I thought. Here's me going on about trust and honesty and I have the biggest secret of all. Squidge. I've fancied Squidge for ages and never told anyone.

'To real friends,' Cat said, putting her hand on the table.

Becca put hers over Cat's. 'To real friends,' she said.

I put my hand over theirs. 'To real friends.'

'So things are better since before assembly?' asked Squidge, sitting down at our table and smiling at me. I felt myself blush even more. Totally honest, I thought . . . That means I have to tell Cat that I fancy her ex-boyfriend. Arghh.

A wave of anxiety flooded through me. How would she react? Maybe best if I keep it quiet and not get into it. I glanced over at her and she gave me a big smile back. What am I thinking? I asked myself. She's not Kaylie. She hasn't got a nasty streak. I can trust her, I know I can. And I have to let her know, by being totally honest with her, that she can trust me.

'So what's all this hand stuff about?' asked Squidge.

'A pledge,' Cat replied. 'To friendship, trust, honesty, no secrets and saying what you really feel to the people you care about.'

Squidge looked deeply into my eyes. I knew he was thinking what I was thinking, and once again, I blushed furiously.

***

In the afternoon break, I saw Cat go into the girls' cloakrooms. It's now or never, I told myself and dived in after her.

She was washing her hands at the sink and looked up when I burst in. 'Hey,' she said. 'It's been a good day, hasn't it?'

'Yeah. But . . . Cat, I have something to tell you,' I blustered.

She dried her hands and leaned back against the sink, ready to listen.

'Er, um . . . I know we said we've got to be honest and stuff, so I'm just going to come out and say it, and if there's even the slightest objection, you have to say. Promise?'

'Yeah. Promise. What is it?'

I took a deep breath. 'Well, it's like . . . there was probably something there the first time. No, um . . . how can I put this? Would you mind if . . . ? No. Er . . .'

Cat laughed. 'Lia, what are trying to say?'

'Um, Squidge.'

Cat looked at me, waiting for me to continue. 'Yeah, Squidge?'

'I like him,' I said.

'Yeah. Everyone likes Squidge.'

'No. I mean, I *like* like him.'

'You like like him? Oh! You *like* like him? As in, fancy?'

'Yeah.'

Cat grinned. 'But that's brilliant. I always knew he liked you. I mean, *like* liked you.'

'Really? And you don't mind?'

'Me? No, course not! No. Me and Squidge, we're long over. It's funny. Even at the beginning, I had a sneaky feeling that he fancied you. Ages ago, he said he thought you were stunning. So, has anything happened?'

I shook my head.

'Has he said anything?'

'Not exactly.'

Suddenly Cat slapped her forehead. 'D'oh. Stupid me. I bet it was Squidge who sent you that Valentine card! Have you got it with you?'

I shook my head.

'Bring it into school tomorrow and I'll tell you. I know his handwriting, even when he tries to disguise it.'

'But really, really, really, you wouldn't mind if I got off with him?'

'Really, really, really,' said Cat. 'In fact, it would make things a lot easier for me, as although he's cool and stuff, I've always been worried about hurting his feelings. I didn't want him to be on his own. I'd love it if he found someone, and even better if it was you. If he was seeing you, I could date other boys without feeling guilty.'

'Date other boys? But what about Ollie?'

'Yeah, Ollie . . .' said Cat. 'I'll see him when he's down

here, but I think we both know that he's not one for the big serious relationship. I'm sure he sees other girls when he's up in London, and I'm not going to get all possessive. I'm not going to let myself go there. I don't want to get burned.'

'He really does like you,' I said, then grinned. 'He always asks after you whenever he phones.'

'Yeah, but does he *like* like me?' teased Cat.

'Yeah, I think he's got a bad case of *like* liking you.'

Cat grinned. 'Good. Let's keep it that way. I know if I got all heavy with him and started demanding that he tells me what's going on with other girls and stuff, he'd be off. No, I want to keep it casual.'

'Treat 'em mean to keep 'em keen?' I asked.

'Sort of. Though I could never be mean to Ollie.'

'I know what you mean,' I said.

Then we both started laughing. 'What do you mean, you know what I mean? That I'm mean, or are you suggesting some other meaning?'

'You're mad, Cat.'

'Mean, mad . . . is there no end to your insults?' She put her fists up in mock fight just as Kaylie came in. 'Hey, Kaylie, do you mean to be mean, or . . . ?'

Kaylie took one look at us, turned on her heel and fled. Cat and I burst out laughing.

Cat shrugged her shoulders. 'I didn't *mean* anything . . .'

'Don't start that again,' I said.

As we made our way back to class, I realised that I hadn't looned about like that for ages. I'd been so careful about everything I said and how I came across, analysing every look and gesture from everyone and wondering if there was anything behind it. It felt so good to feel carefree again. Plus, now I knew that Cat wouldn't mind about Squidge. The future was beginning to look very promising.

17 White Flag

AFTER SCHOOL, we all piled back to Cat's house.

'I think we should celebrate,' said Cat, going into their kitchen and straight to the fridge. 'Who wants a scone, and oh . . . there's a tub of Cornish cream. Who wants a cream tea?'

'Well, we do live in Cornwall,' said Becca. 'When in Cornwall, do as the Cornish do.'

'Do you have strawberrry jam?' I asked.

Cat rummaged in the fridge and produced a pot of jam, which she put on the table. 'We do.'

Becca read the label. 'Straight from Widdecombe's Farm and on to our hips. Oh, what the hell? It's a celebration.'

Cat rolled her eyes. 'I don't know why you worry about your weight so much. You're just right.'

'Just right for the Teletubbies, you mean.'

I laughed. Becca looks great, but thinks that she's big. She's mad. She's got a great figure.

Five minutes later, just as we were tucking into freshly baked scones oozing with jam and cream, my mobile bleeped that there was a text message. I wiped the crumbs off my hands and checked the message.

'It's from Kaylie. It says, if I dare go to any of the teachers about her, my life won't be worth living.' I laughed. 'How pathetic is that?'

'Oooh scary,' said Cat, putting her hand on her heart and feigning a faint. 'Bite me.'

'Hmm,' said Becca. 'Warning you off going to the teachers. She was obviously rattled by Miss Segal's class. What should we do?'

'Nothing,' I said. 'I honestly don't think it's worth it. She knows what she's done and so does most of our class now. In fact, I wouldn't be surprised if the table turns and she finds people ganging up against her now that they realise that they're not alone.'

'Serve her right if they do,' said Becca.

'Yeah. But you know what, life's too short. I should have listened to Dad. He told me that at one point in his life, the press gave him a hard time. He said it took him years to learn just to leave it. Not retaliate, not to try and put the story straight, just leave it. That's what I'd like to do. She probably only wants a reaction – you know, to see that she's upset me or scared me. That's what gives her the power. But if she doesn't get the reaction she expects, no power. Anyway, I've really had enough of it all . . .'

'Oh, you mustn't leave, Lia,' said Cat. 'Please don't talk about going back to your old school again.'

'Don't worry, I won't. No. Enough of all the bad feelings. I don't want revenge or to get back at her, or to give her a taste of her own medicine, or anything. I just want it all to stop. She leaves me alone, I leave her alone.'

'So, what do we do, then? Wave a white flag to say we don't want to do battle?'

I thought for a moment. 'Actually, that's not a bad idea. Let's send her one more e-mail,' I said.

'What?! After what happened last time?' asked Becca. 'You're mad.'

'What kind of e-mail?' asked Cat.

'Sort of last chance kind of thing . . .'

Becca sighed. 'You're far too forgiving, Lia.'

'No, I'm not. Not forgiving. I'll never forget what she's done, but I do want this to be the end of it now. *Finito. Kaput.*'

'Suit yourself,' said Becca. 'But I think you're mad. You just said what your dad said. Don't engage. Don't have anything to do with bullies.'

'I won't after today, but I just want it to end on a positive note – not with her having the last word with that stupid threat of hers. I want to let her know that I'm not scared and that I'm not in to waging some stupid battle either. We've got years left at school. I want her to be clear about the way it's going to be with me.'

Cat looked at Becca. 'Makes sense.'

After we'd finished tea, we went into Cat's dad's study and turned on the computer.

'Sign it from all of us so that she knows that we're here with you,' said Cat. 'But what shall we say?'

'Dear Kaylie, get lost, you stupid loser,' said Becca.

'Tempting,' I said, 'but . . . can I write it, then if you agree, we'll send it?'

'Course,' said Cat then made way for me to sit down.

Dear Kaylie,

First, your threats don't scare me. In fact, I think they're pretty pathetic. Second, I'm well aware that you might send this round our class again, but who cares? Do what you like. I never wanted any trouble between us and I'm prepared to put it all behind me. I know that after today, a lot of girls are ready to gang up against you, but I think this whole thing should stop here, for good. I propose that tomorrow morning, we meet before assembly and we go in together and show our year that we are all OK and have resolved our differences. I'm not

suggesting that we become friends, as that will
never happen, but I don't want any more crap at
school.

   I'll be outside the school gate at 8.55. The
choice is yours.

Li@ @xford.

Cat leaned over my shoulder and typed in: And C@t and
Becc@.

'You sure you want to send it?' asked Becca when she'd
finished reading it.

I nodded.

Cat leaned over and pressed the 'Send' button.

Kiss

THE NEXT morning, I got up early and put on my favourite track. It's called 'Don't Panic' by Coldplay and it always makes me feel really up and in a good mood. I haven't played it for weeks, but as the words to the song echoed around my bedroom, I found myself singing along. 'We live in a beautiful world . . .'

Mum knocked on my door, then came in and sat on the end of the bed. 'You're feeling happy today. What's happening?'

'I have decided to be myself,' I said.

'Ah,' said Mum. 'Good. At least, I think it is. And what exactly does this entail?'

I sat next to her. 'It means that I'm no longer going to hide who I am or who my family are. In fact, I wondered if you could give me a lift to school today?'

'In Meena's car?'

'Nope. In your gorgeous Porsche.'

Mum laughed. 'So what happened to low-key?'

'Not me,' I said. 'That was last month. I've realised we are what we are. I am who I am. I can't spend my whole life pretending to be something I'm not. I'm Lia Axford, my dad's a rock star and I'm proud of it. I've spent so much time apologising for the fact that we live well and I have nice things. Well, I'm going to enjoy it from now on. Why not?'

'Why not, indeed,' said Mum. 'So what's brought on this change?'

'Long story. Just . . . I've realised that I might be quiet, but I'm not invisible. Nope. I'm going to be who I am and happy about it.'

Mum smiled. 'Excellent. Now get a move on or we're going to be late.'

When she'd gone, I got my Cartier watch out of its box and put it back on my wrist. Then I found my Valentine's card and put it in my rucksack ready to show Cat. I picked my best pair of jeans and DKNY T-shirt and put them on. Then I applied a little mascara, a little lip-gloss, a squirt of Cristalle and I was ready.

Cat and Becca were waiting for me at the school gates when Mum and I drew up. Cat whistled when I got out the car.

'Hubba hubba,' she said as Mum hooted, then drove off. 'You look great. You haven't worn your hair loose like that for ages.

'Thanks . . .' I said as I looked around. 'Any sign of Kaylie?'

'Not yet,' said Becca.

I pulled out the Valentine's card and showed it to Cat. She took one look and grinned. 'Definitely,' she said. 'Squidge always was rubbish at trying to disguise his handwriting.'

I smiled back at her. I was really chuffed that it was from Squidge. All that time he'd liked me and had never said a word.

'Hmmm, you and Squidge, huh?' said Becca. 'Cat told me all about it. I think it's brilliant.'

I grinned. 'So do I.'

After that, we stood and waited. And waited. Finally the school bell went for assembly.

'She's not going to show, is she?' I said.

Becca shook her head. 'Didn't think she would.'

'Do you mind?' asked Cat

'Not at all,' I said, and I meant it. 'Her loss. Now we'd better run.'

We made it into the hall just in time and lined up with the others in our class. There was no sign of Kaylie. It was only when we were going into our first lesson that Cat spotted her. With the Clones as usual, and they were going into class. It didn't bother me one bit that she hadn't shown up at the gates. I'd waved the white flag and she'd chosen to ignore it. Fine by me. While we waited for Mr Riley, our maths teacher, to arrive, Cat, Becca and I went over to chat to Laura, Sunita and Tina on the opposite side of the room from the Clones.

'Cat told us about the e-mail, Lia,' said Sunita. 'Good for you. But no show, huh?'

'No show. But no worries either,' I said. 'I couldn't give a toss.'

'I think she could,' said Laura, glancing over at Kaylie. 'She looks dreadful, like she hasn't slept for a week.'

'Good,' said Tina. 'Now she knows how it feels.'

'I think you're right, though,' said Laura. 'It's not that I'm scared of her or anything any more, but I don't want to get into a revenge thing. Like you, I want to leave it and get on with life. Stick with the friends I've got and not think about her. I hate all that bad vibe stuff.'

Excellent, I thought as I looked around. There are some really nice girls in our year and I resolved to invite them over and get to know them better.

'OK, take your places,' said Mr Riley as he came in through the door.

As the morning classes went on, I glanced over at Kaylie a few times, but she kept her head down through the whole lesson, like she didn't want to look at anyone. She did look terrible, but it was her choice not to have turned up at the gates and go into assembly with us. I felt totally indifferent about it. No loss. She didn't want to change, but I did. I felt like the whole ordeal had made me stronger, firmer in my resolve to be true to myself and to my friends, and to spend time getting to know people I actually liked. For the time being, Kaylie's campaign was over and if she ever started up again, she couldn't touch me.

When school ended that day, I went out to wait for my lift home as usual. As I was standing at the pick-up point, my mobile bleeped. Oh, here we go, I thought as I checked the text message. Maybe Kaylie wants to have one last go at me . . . But it wasn't from her. It was from Squidge.

'Do u want to meet l8r?' it said.

I texted back. 'Yes.'

'Meet me at the bttm of ur drive at 7.'

'OK.'

An amazing feeling of anticipation fluttered in my stomach as I tried to envisage what he might want.

He arrived to pick me up on his battered old moped.

'So, where are we going?' I asked as I climbed on the back.

'Rame Head,' he answered.

'But it's dark.'

'I know.'

We rode up the lanes in silence and I wondered why he'd want to go up there at this time. We wouldn't be able to see the amazing view. Not that I really minded. I was alone with Squidge and that was enough for me.

Ten minutes later, Squidge parked his moped in the field near the peninsula, then he unhooked his rucksack from the back.

'What's in there?' I asked. 'It looks really heavy.'

'You'll see,' he said, pulling out a parka jacket. 'Here, put this on. It might be cold up there.'

I put on the coat over my jacket and Squidge led the way with his torch. We trudged across the field that led to the small hill where the church was, then began the ascent up the wooden steps to the church at the top.

'Careful,' said Squidge, shining his torch so that I could see. 'Hold on to the banister.'

'Don't worry, I am,' I said. Apart from the torch light, it was very black out there, as there are no electric lights or lampposts, but strangely, I didn't feel frightened – only intrigued. I looked up at the sky. It was a clear night and I could see a million stars.

When we got to the top, Squidge led me to the side of the church. 'OK, stay here and close your eyes, and I'll tell you when to open them.'

I did as I was told. 'Good job I trust you,' I said.

Squidge did a maniacal laugh, then I heard him walk into the church. What on earth could he be doing? I wondered.

A short time later, he came back out and took my hand. 'OK, you can come now, but don't open your eyes yet.'

He led me around the side of the church, then inside. 'OK,' he said, 'you can open your eyes now.'

I opened my eyes and gasped. 'Wow! It's beautiful.'

The church is tiny – only three metres by four, with three gaps in the walls where once there were probably windows. Inside, it is all grey stone – even the floor. If there was ever any tiling on the floor, it's long gone. Usually, it's cold and damp in there, but this night, it looked like the most magical place on earth. What Squidge had been carrying in his bag were candles and nightlights. Loads of them. He'd placed them all around the floor and on the window ledges and they glowed a soft, golden light.

'This is what it must have been like in ancient times,' said Squidge. 'Imagine coming up to a service here from the village before there was any electric lighting.'

'Amazing,' I said. 'An amazing atmosphere. Like Christmas.'

Squidge produced a flask from his bag. 'And supplies,' he

said. 'I thought we might want something warm, so, cup of tea, vicar?'

I laughed and took the cup he was offering me.

'Actually, it's hot chocolate,' he said. 'Much nicer than tea.'

'So what made you do this, Squidge?'

He shrugged. 'Every time I come here, it feels special. Energising. The locals say that a lot of very powerful ley lines converge here . . .'

'What are ley lines?'

'They're supposed to be prehistoric tracks, joining prominent points on the landscape – likes churches and burial grounds. Stonehenge is on a ley line so are the Stone Circles and the Standing Stones. I suppose you could say that in the same way that rivers carry water, these ley lines carry good energy, which is probably why people used to come to them to worship in ancient times. You know, to soak up the good vibes. Anyway, I always wanted to come up here at night. I've often tried to imagine how it must have been in the old days, so I thought I'd recreate it.'

I looked around at the tiny church bathed in the soft glow of the candles and nightlights. 'Totally magical,' I said. 'Very good energy. I've always felt that too whenever I've come up here. It's like my battery gets charged, if you know what I mean.'

He nodded. 'I plan to film something up here one day. Maybe some scene from the past. You can have a lead role if you like.'

'God. I can't act for toffee. In fact, the only time I got a lead part was when I was five. I was in the Nativity play as Mary and totally forgot my lines. Since then I've been out of the way in the chorus.'

'Well, you *were* only five,' said Squidge. 'And I bet you were very cute. I was in a Nativity play as well when I was little. I played a donkey.'

I laughed. 'Have you always been so sure of what you want to do? You know, to direct films?'

Squidge nodded again. 'Sort of. I mean, I started out taking photos, then Dad got me a video camera and it evolved from there.'

'You've never wanted to act, then – always direct?'

'Oh yes, that way I get to cast the movie and pick the locations and so on. Location is so important, it has to be the right place for the right moment in a film.'

'And what is this kind of location right for?' I asked. In my mind, it was perfect for a romantic scene. I wondered if he thought the same.

Squidge smiled a half-smile, looked full into my eyes and leaned closer to me. I felt my chest tighten and for a moment I thought he was going to kiss me. But he leaned away and the moment was over. 'Something and someone very special,' he said. 'But it's not just for films that you choose locations.'

'What do you mean?'

'I guess having got interested in making films has made me think about a lot of things. The parallels in life. Life is what you make it, just as a film is what the director makes it.'

'Explain.'

'I see my life like I'm making a film. It's like, the camera starts rolling the moment you're born and it films your perspective on life – a view that's totally unique in the universe. Your view. But that's not all. In a film there's a leading lady, a leading man, sometimes a baddie, parts for extras and so on. In your life, you're making *your* film. You've got the lead part, like I've got the lead part in mine. You had a baddie in yours, Kaylie O'Horrible. Thing is, we can choose how the script goes. I'm realising it more and more. Whether we're going to play a hero, a heroine or someone who loses it all. It's choice, just as it is in a script. You make up your own dialogue, your own responses and so on. In your own film, you are the writer, the . . .'

I laughed. 'I get it – the writer, director and producer. At the end, the credits will come up: *My life, starring Lia Axford, Cat Kennedy, Becca Howard . . .*'

'Yeah, exactly. You chose to cast them as friends,' said

Squidge. 'You choose the locations as well, the plot lines, the love interests, the lot.'

'I like that. Creator of my own movie.'

'And the cameras are rolling now,' continued Squidge, 'behind your eyes, seeing it all from your point of view, so you get to be cameraman as well. You choose what to focus on, what details to zoom in and out on, et cetera.'

Well, I'm zooming in on your mouth at the moment, I thought. Everyone at school thinks that Jonno is the best-looking boy in school – well, I prefer Squidge. His face is far more interesting. But it's not just his face, I thought, watching him. It's the way his face lights up when he talks. And he has great style. I love the long black leather coat he wears. It makes him look so cool. Choice, he said. Was it my choice that Kaylie was so horrible to me? Maybe it was, partly, because I fell into playing a part in *her* film and she had chosen me to play the part of a victim. Not any more, pal. I'm taking back control of *my* movie and I want a better role.

'You're staring at me,' said Squidge, smiling.

'Oh, sorry, I was just thinking . . .'

'About what?'

'About choice. I've had such a weird time lately. I was thinking that I didn't feel I had much choice in it. But you're right, I did. I chose how I responded to things. Like that saying – you can either sink or swim. I was sinking for a while back there and now I've chosen to swim. I was letting Kaylie have a major part in my movie, and now,' I laughed, 'she's sacked. I don't want her in the film at all. She can be an extra in the background school scenes. And definitely *no* dialogue.'

'Good,' said Squidge.

'It's funny, because the whole thing with her started after that game of Truth, Dare, Kiss or Promise,' I said. 'Remember on Valentine's Day, when Becca told us all we had to kiss someone and she told me I had to kiss Jonno?'

Squidge's face clouded for a moment. 'Oh yeah, your leading man. How's that going?'

'Ah. I think I'm going to do a recast. I'm the director of my movie. I can do that, can't I?'

Squidge smiled again. 'Sure. Does Jonno know that he's been made redundant yet?'

I shook my head. 'Haven't written the dialogue for that scene yet, but I'm going to work on it over the next few days and tell him next time I see him.'

After this evening, I was more sure than ever that I had to end it with Jonno. I'd only been with Squidge a short while, but he was so interesting. He really thought about things. And not *one* mention of football.

'But forget Jonno for a moment. Thinking back to Valentine's night, you never fulfilled the kiss dare. You said you were going to do it in your own time.'

Squidge was quiet for a moment. 'I will when the time is right.'

I *really* wanted him to kiss me, like I've never felt before. 'And when do you think that will be?'

Squidge did this amazing thing. He smiled with his eyes, then he looked at the floor. 'Right girl, right time,' he said, then looked up into my eyes. 'You can't hurry it. It's like an avocado pear – if you bite into it too soon, it doesn't taste as good as when it's ripened.'

I felt my stomach flip over. If he'd been waiting for me, then I was ready. No doubt about it – I'd never felt this way about a boy, *ever* – not even Ollie's friend, Michael. This felt different. Special. I felt so alive. Hyper, like I'd drunk ten cups of coffee, yet strangely calm at the same time. Life is what you make it, Squidge had said. You make the choices about how you want your movie to turn out. Well, I choose not to be so timid any more, I thought. I want a more fun role in my own film. But is *he* ready to play the next scene? As Squidge continued to look into my eyes, I wondered how to speed up the process.

'Well, winter's over,' I said. 'Spring is on its way, then summer. Good times for things to ripen, I'd say.'

I took a deep breath, took a step towards him and gently put my arms around his neck. He slid his hands around my waist and pulled me close, then . . .

Cue slushy soundtrack as the camera pulls away to fade out.

The End.

Well, it's my film. I can do that. And I think most people can guess what happened next. . .

Find out more at www.piccadillypress.co.uk
Join Cathy's Club at www.cathyhopkins.com

Cathy Hopkins

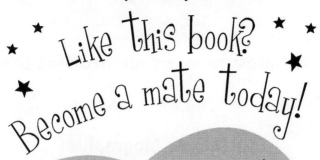

Like this book?
Become a mate today!

Join CATHY'S CLUB and be the first to get the lowdown on the LATEST NEWS, BOOKS and FAB COMPETITIONS straight to your mobile and e-mail.

PLUS there's a FREE MOBILE WALLPAPER when you sign up! What are you waiting for?

Simply text MATE plus your date of birth (ddmmyyyy) to 60022 now! Or go to www.cathyhopkins.com and sign up online.

Once you've signed up keep your eyes peeled for exclusive chapter previews, cool downloads, freebies and heaps more fun stuff all coming your way.

www.piccadillypress.co.uk

☆ The latest news on forthcoming books

☆ Chapter previews

☆ Author biographies

☆ Fun quizzes

☆ Reader reviews

☆ Competitions and fab prizes

☆ Book features and cool downloads

☆ And much, much more . . .

Log on and check it out!

Piccadilly Press

☆